AF655837

Short Stories
from
Devayana
Third Epic of India

Book-2

Short Stories

from

Devayana

Third Epic of India

Book - 2

Amita Nathwani
Maggie Voysey Paun

MOONLIGHT BOOKS

Short Stories from Devayana Book-2

FIRST EDITION: 2020

ISBN PB: 978-81-944508-2-5
ISBN EBOOK: 978-81-944508-3-2

Published by
MOONLIGHT BOOKS
20 Ekjot Apartment, Pitampura, Delhi-110034, India
Email: moonlightbooks2016@gmail.com
www.moonlightbooks.in

Printed by Replika Press Pvt. Ltd., India

Contents

OTHER BOOKS BY AMITA NATHWANI

◈ Glimpses of Devayana
◈ The Voice of the Rsis
◈ Tales from the Devayana
◈ Devayan Vols. (I – XI)

An epic always precedes the changing of an age in India. This is apparent from the past. Before the passage from the Silver to the Bronze Age, Ramayana was recorded. Mahabharata was written before the transition from the Bronze to the Iron Age. Now with the Iron Age coming to an end, and with the Golden Age approaching, a new epic, Devayan, has manifested.

Devayan, unlike the former two epics, does not only reveal to us the approaching Golden Age. Instead it describes the complete human cycle of 26,000 years covering the Golden, the Silver, the Bronze and the Iron Ages. It consists of twelve volumes, with a thousand pages each, divided into thirty-two books, written in the Anushthupa metre, the classical Indian epic metre. It deals with the "origin and the creation of the universe"; the complete history of the world during the Four Ages, including the approaching Golden Age. This is the age of the Supramental consciousness as envisaged by Sri Aurobindo. Man will evolve into a being with a totally new and divine consciousness based upon the Vedic truths. The great Indian tradition lives on.

For Purchase, kindly contact at :
Email : amita.nathwani@gmail.com,
nilesh.nathwani@aon.at
Website : www.devayan.net

Introduction

Time as we know in our daily life runs in a straight line. We know our past, we live at every moment through the present and the future is something that we only guess about and let our imagination run wild. There is however another theory, that time is cyclical and it takes the shape of repeating after every 26,000 years. This view is explained in our old scriptures and now in the third epic of India, the Devayan.

The stories in this book are taken from the Devayana, the third epic of India which was written down by Dr Hajari, a young follower of the famous Yogi, Sri Aurobindo. These stories are shorter and more concise version of the translations that are included in More Tales from the Devayana - from the epic. It tells the story of the Four Ages of Time: the Treta Yuga (Silver Age), Dwapara Yuga (Bronze Age), Kali Yuga (Iron Age, in which we live) and the Satya Yuga or the Golden Age.

The epic consists of more than twelve thousand pages of poetry divided into twelve volumes. First written in Bengali, it has been transcribed into Hindi/Sanskrit by Amita Nathwani, whose mother Dr Indira Sardana was a devotee in the Aurobindo Ashram in Pondicherry on the eastern coast of India. She had a serious heart condition which was healed by Dr Hajari, a homeopathic doctor, and when she learnt of the Devayana she determined to make its revelations known to a wider world.

This second selection of stories spans the time between the origins of creation through the threat to, and defeat of, the reign of truth on earth and the struggle to restore it. The world is still in the thrall of Kali Yuga but as told in the last story, and as foretold in ancient scriptures, the Satya Yuga or the Age of Truth will return.

☆☆☆☆☆

Before Creation
The Birth of Sound[1]

One day, a long time ago, Rishi Kakshivan was walking with Satyadeva, the son of Rishi Abhivarta, when suddenly they heard a tremendous explosion. It was as if winds from a hundred thousand storms were blowing at the same time. There came another unbelievably loud bang like the noise of a hundred thunderbolts.

'Whatever is that?' asked Satyadeva.

Kakshivan bent closer to make himself heard. "Listen to me, and I will tell you all I know about sound and the formation of words," he began. "Together with Ambhrini, Aptya Rishi created a daughter, Vak, who was destined to marry the Sun God. Vak had undertaken many yogic austerities until the eternal sound, *Om*, was born from her womb. Then, together with the Sun God she created fourteen immortal and powerful sons who, illuminated by their father's power, shone brightly. From their mother they obtained the knowledge of sound. Each of them had forty sons, who also created yet more sounds, their aim being to spread and magnify the Truth.

---

[1]Devayan Vol. I/Brahma Kalpa/Deva Mandal/Kakshi Varga/Chapter 22-23/pages 276-280

"The sounds continued to multiply until they became so many that they formed the Ocean of Sound, called the Aksharap. From this, letters were created out of which consonants and vowels took birth. There were myriads of them throughout the ocean. Taken all together, they were called the Aksharabrahman, the sound as the Creator. The powerful verses, Rik, from the Rigveda; Sama, from the Samaveda; Yajat from the Yajurveda; and the Atharvan from the Atharvaveda, were asked to reside in Akshara brahman to control and propel these letters towards Truth.

"Seeing this great manifestation of Truth, Nakta, the deepest darkness, was furious. He could not bear the pressure that this light of Truth caused in Brahma's creation. In order to sully its purity, he kidnapped Vak, made her his captive and managed to impregnate her. When he heard of Vak's kidnapping, Brahma was enraged and loudly summoned Nakta.

'You dared to kidnap Vak?' Thundered Brahma. 'Bring her to me immediately.'

"Nakta trembled with fear and terror. He freed Vak immediately; and then, to save himself, fled directly to the netherworlds, to hell, to hide in its furthest corner.

"Full of pain and sorrow, Vak presented herself in front of the Creator and told him that not only had Nakta kidnapped, but he had also impregnated her. On hearing this, the Creator was furious. He tried without success to find Nakta and ordered Vak to abort the foetus without delay. She pleaded that it was too soon, and that the time was not right, but still she obeyed and, as a result, a very strange creature was born.

"Its face was like a horse, with two ears, but its tongue was like a snake. It had a long body also like a snake, but it had hundreds of thousands of tails and two big wings which were much bigger than the body. Emitting light, it moved in a circular fashion.

"When he saw the new creation, the Creator laughed and said that it looked so strange that he would have to take care of it himself. He provided food to give it strength to survive and because of its movement called it Kalachakra, the Wheel of Time.

'Listen Kalachakra,' he said. 'Your task will be to support the Ocean of Sound on your head; and, on your body and tails, the three planes of existence, the Bhur, Bhuvar and the Swar; the material, the vital and the mental planes. You will, at all times, remain in space. When creation multiplies, your power will also increase. At that time, you will show your accumulated power with a loud noise and your thunder will be heard in the east of the huge Ocean of Sound as you support it from below.'"

Satyadeva was very happy to hear this explanation but he still wanted to know how Vak purified herself. Kakshivan did not know so he took Satyadeva to his father, Dirghtama, who knew everything about Vak's penance. But when they reached the place where Dirghtama was, they were astounded by what he told them.

"Vak brought into this world the Lord of Truth to spread the light of Truth in the furthest corners of the world," said Dirghtama. "His name is Satyadeva and he will remove the suffering and pain caused by Kali, the Lord of the Iron Age. He will influence birth and actions in the world. He, himself, will take a divine form. My son, look at your companion. He is the Deva, the Lord of Truth. He is visiting many areas in the world. Today, due to my yogic austerities, he has come here, so that I could demonstrate to him the Ocean of Sound. With this, my tapasya has come to an end."

☆☆☆☆☆

The Human Being-Struggle Between Gods and Demons Through the Ages[2]

Through aeons of Creation the perfect being in which the Gods could dwell, had still not been found. Many living beings had been created but, from the smallest to the biggest, none were acceptable to them. However, when they saw the first human being, the Gods were satisfied and entered into it, telling Manu to stop his work of creation. Their period of waiting and watching from afar had come to an end.

Each found his or her own place from which to spread their divine influence in the world. The Sun God, Surya, resided in the eyes to provide the vision of Truth; and in the ears, Rudra. On the forehead, between the two eyebrows, Brihaspati, the Guru of the Gods took his place; below the throat was Chandra, the Moon God; in the abdomen was Mitra-Varun. In the genitals was Yama, the God of Justice; and in the legs, the twin Ashwinis. Lord Vishnu was in the heart; Lord Brahma

[2]Devayan Volume 10/Rudra Kalpa/Aptya Mandala/Rishi Varga/chapter 31-34/pages 2236-2243;

Devayan/Volume 9/Rudra Kalpa/Pratishta Mandala/Amar Varga/chapter 24/1960-1961

in the navel; and, on the top of the head, was Lord Indra. The Wind God, Vayu, gave both arms his force; while Lord Shiva, together with his Shakti, resided in the Muladhara, the lowermost point of the body. In this way, the Gods established themselves in the human body.

This arrangement lasted for a while but, all too soon, Diti, the Demon Mother, began to conspire with her offspring, the Asuras, or demons, to hinder this divine plan. They, too, wanted power over human beings and requested Rishi Kashyap, the Creator, to create a new being where they could have their own sphere of influence. He told them that it was not necessary, as they and the Devas were brothers and they should live in peace together; but still the Asuras insisted upon their stake in half of this new creation.

And so the Gods remained in the part of the body above the navel, which was considered to be the heavens, while Diti and her sons were allocated the lower part of the body, from the knees to the feet, the nether world. The middle area, between the navel and the knees, was the mortal world, the area for the satisfaction of desires and enjoyment, where there began a continuous struggle between the Gods and the Asuras for control.

To assist in this work, the powers of the Rishis; which had been created through their own effort and through their long yogic austerities, also entered into the human body. Each divided their Shakti, power, into two parts - one the higher and the other the lower one, and gave these to the higher and the lower areas, controlled by Aditi and Diti. For example, Rishi Gautam's power, Ahalya, the divine power, was given to Aditi while Halya, the undivine power, was given to Diti, the Demon Mother. Rishi Atri's power, Anusuya, ascended in the upper part to assist Aditi and to support the Gods, while the lower force, Irsha, jealousy, joined forces with Diti to manage the lower forces in the body. Rishi Kanva gave to Aditi, his power Kanaa that gives memory to man; and Bhrama (doubt) to women in their lower parts. (This power, later on joined hands with Kali, and thus many a time, women managed to create doubts and hindrances in choosing the right way). In this way, the Gods and the Demons influenced human beings.

Rishi Vashishta's power Arundhati assisted Aditi; while Dhuti, the demonic power, joined together with Diti to control and help the demonic forces. Mitra's power, Mitra, amity, was under the suzerainty of Aditi, the Mother of the Gods; while Rishtta, destruction, went to Diti to assist the Demons. Rishi Bhardawaj's power Riti, the right direction, joined hands with Aditi; while Vipriti, the opposite force, aided Diti in the lower areas.

In man, knowledge entered in the higher parts of the body, under the divine influence, while there was ignorance in their lower areas. In women, in the higher parts, Usha Sangya, the power of the Sun God prevailed, while in the lower areas, attachment made its place. In the middle portion of the women, a ceremonial sacrifice took its place, in which the men, like the priest took the role of organising this daily ceremony, which was like a continuing worship. Many Rishis' sons took this responsibility and undertook a daily ceremonial sacrifice, to please and invoke the Gods. In this way, men and women worshipped the divine in their life and made this world into heaven.

The Golden Age

Human beings remained in this divine state for a long period of time. Man said: "I am the Deva, influencing the world; I am the eternal Brahma; I am Rudra; I am Vishnu; I am Indra, the Leader of the Gods. I am Agni, the God of Fire; I am the powerful Vayu, the Wind God; I am Yama, the one who dispenses justice; I am Mitra, who promotes friendship all around. I am the Ashwinis, who heal everything. I am the Sun God; I am Bhaga, promoting joy within and without; I am Aryaman; I am Twasta. It is me who is Brihaspati, the Guru of the Gods. I am the Chandra, the Moon God; I am the mighty Pusha; I am the Seven Rishis. The mighty Sons of the Rishis are the Priests in my body."

Gaining a similar knowledge, women told their menfolk: "You are all these things but I am the Power, the Shakti. Accept this offering from my complete body."

Then man was filled with delight and clasped woman to his chest saying: "You are a Goddess. Reside in me as the divine power and bring my emotions to light."

On hearing these words, the woman's body became full of joy and she invited the man to live as her God, in her life. With the presence of the Gods, the human body became full of health and beauty and both men and women radiated divine light from their countenances.

The Iron Age

Seeing this joy and happiness, the demons were filled with jealousy and rage and they forced their way also into the higher part of the human body in the Kaliyuga, the Iron Age. With Shukracharya controlling the mind, and with Shani and Kali's powerful force, mankind's innate knowledge was covered with a layer of ignorance and the sense organs became deluded.

While the Gods influence humans through their inner being, Kali as the Leader of the Age influences them from outside. When the Gods withdraw, or they become inactive, people start to doubt their existence or they start to believe that they are indifferent to mere humans. They believe that they cannot help them. Therefore, there seems no point in offering prayer, and religion focuses merely on rituals and other external matters. Money gains in importance, and achieving material comfort becomes the main goal of human life.

On observing that it is their own body that acts, and that their eyes see the outside world, humanity thinks that they are the one who is doing the action. Seeing that this face, this mouth is their own through which they consume food, human beings start thinking that they themselves are in sole control. They believe only what their mind tells them is true and take great pride in their intelligence. However, since the sole responsibility for their well-being depends upon their own efforts, their minds become full of worries about needs that have to be constantly satisfied. In these ways, the human mind operates in a very different manner to how it did in the Golden Age.

Kali is always opposed to the Gods. Under his influence humanity becomes immersed in an all-encompassing selfishness and the pursuit of personal enjoyment. Not only that, he convinces people that they are insignificant, a miniscule and insignificant part of the vast universe without having the ability to change their situation. Weak, apathetic and lacking in confidence, they come to believe that there is no point in even trying and, with the passing of time, they are forced to observe helplessly as they start losing their keen senses and faculties. Their vision begins to dim, their hearing becomes weak. Moreover, they find difficulties in walking and performing the most mundane activities.

And always, there is the fear of Death which conquers each and every human being. With minds darkened with disbelief, their divine origin remains hidden, and there seems to be no escape from the gloomiest despair.

End of Kali Yuga

Observing from afar the unending misery of life on earth, Satyadeva, the Lord of Truth, asked Surya how the age of Kali might be ended. Surya, the Sun God, answered, "The condition of the world will be very sad at this time. There will be no belief in Gods and in the divine Dharma, the true religion will vanish completely from the earth. No offerings will be made to the Gods and there will be no efforts to reach divinity. Belief will be non-existent, trust will vanish and each will suspect the other. It will go so far that humans will not even trust their own parents, brothers and sisters.

"Additionally, a great fear will pervade in the whole world. Strife and conflicts will be everywhere; between people, countries, and regions and even between the various religions. It will spread to all countries, reaching each and every family and home. This will be the end of Time and only then will your work commence. Your task will be mainly to explain the various aspects and dangers of darkness and ignorance, and Mitra's to tell you the right path to follow and the correct moment at which to begin. He will accompany you in your great deeds."

Then, Mitra appeared and told Satyadeva that he should now re-establish the broken connection between heaven and earth and bind them close together.

"Evil has made so many divisions in the world," he said. "In your time, Satyadeva, there was divine unity. The entire creation was one unit. As soon as you left this world, the earth and the heavens were rent apart. This occurred during the Silver Age, the Treta Yuga. After this Age ended, the world was divided into even smaller parts and human beings became alienated. In the Dwapara Yuga, it was due to racial differences. People started to think those coming from other races were different from them, when basically they were one. At the end of the Dwapara Yuga, the full impact of Kali manifested and conflicts arose between different parts of the world and different religions. With this, came also fights in each family, in each home.

"Oh Lord, remove all these barriers between human beings and bring back unity to the entire world. The Gods have always promoted different qualities among human beings but they lived in peace together; still the Creator, the mighty Brahma, was present in everyone. Worshipping him, we held our daily ceremonial sacrifice, *yajna*, and offered our prayers to the One that existed everywhere and in everything. Ensure that with *yajna*, prayers to the divine will start again. As soon as that is achieved, Gods will once again come to make their place in each and every person. Then Kali's evil Age, the Kali Yuga will be banished completely from the world."

☆☆☆☆☆

When Krishna Rescued Rukmini[3]

When Lord Krishna heard that a Brahmin had come from the distant city of Vidarbha with an urgent message from King Bhishmak, he was very surprised. As far as he knew, there was no outstanding business with Vidharbha. He hurried to his palace to meet the Brahmin.

Having welcomed the venerable old man and made him comfortable, he asked him the reason for his visit. The Brahmin remained quiet for a while, pondering how best to present the issue. Then he looked up at Krishna with a beseeching expression and murmured that he needed to talk with him privately. Krishna's curiosity grew. He did not know the Brahmin's reason for secrecy but respected his wishes and, taking him by the hand, led him to a smaller room and once there, he repeated his question.

The old man was very happy to see Lord Krishna alone. When Krishna had held his hand, his whole body had vibrated with joy, as if it had received an immense jolt of energy. He bowed down in front of Krishna. "Oh Krishna, you are indeed the Lord of the entire Creation,"

[3]Devayan Vol. 8/Rudra Kalpa/Krishna Mandal/Bhagawata Purana/Rajya Skandha/Chapter 50-54/pages 246-255

he said. "I have always seen your luminous face in my mind when I meditate. Please bless me." Deeply moved, he began to cry and washed Krishna's feet with his tears. Only after some time could he bring himself under control.

"Esteemed Brahmin," Krishna said, "please tell me the real reason why you undertook such a long journey to Dwarka. There must be something important and serious behind your visit."

"Now that I have no more doubts about you, I shall explain," said the Brahmin. "In Vidarbha, our Princess Rukmini had a very profound spiritual experience. She had gone into a deep meditation and came to know of your birth in this world. In fact, she described your appearance to me in minute details. Seeing you in front of me, I am fully convinced that what she experienced was true. The Princess told me to look for the dark colour of your skin and your beautiful wide eyes. She said that your nose was long, the expression on your face forever smiling. She added, 'Oh Brahmin, Krishna is very strong. He has a high forehead, a broad chest and he looks as strong as a lion. His legs are powerful with feet like lotuses. Believe me, that in Dwarka at present, the Lord of the World has descended.'

"It was she who asked me to go urgently to Dwarka and give this letter into your hands without anyone becoming aware of it. She told me to first meet you and be completely sure that you were the person whom she saw in her vision. Her message is: 'Oh Lord, your Lakshmi is in Vidarbha and is being troubled by evil persons. O Vishnu, please hurry and save her from this dire condition.'"

"But tell me, what is the problem?" Krishna demanded. "What is this situation that your Princess is facing?"

The Brahmin handed a letter to Krishna who, with mounting concern, read Rukmini's words. 'I bow down before you, O Divine Madhusudan. I recall our last conversation in heaven. You told me of the difficult conditions prevalent on the earth where the demons and negative forces were gaining the upper hand. For this reason, you decided to take birth in Mathura and you told me to be born in the royal family of Vidarbha. We both came down from the higher worlds and I took birth in the home of King Bhishmak. I am your Lakshmi. Recently, I have come to know about some very disturbing developments that I must urgently share with you.

'While meditating, I have learnt details of your life. How you lived in Vraja as a child and were happy amongst the Gopis. I heard then that you went to Mathura and destroyed Kansa, one of the evil demons that you had wanted to eliminate from the world. Subsequently, you fought many wars with the powerful Jarasandha whom in the end you managed to defeat, and later you established your reign in the island of Dwarka where the ocean protects you. During all this time, I was waiting for a sign from you. I believed that you would come to meet me.

'Now, I am writing to beseech you to come urgently and rescue me for I am in extreme danger. Lately your cousin, the evil Shishupala, the King of Chedi, came to my father and begged him for my hand in marriage and my father Bhishmak has agreed. My brother Rukmi, being a very close friend of his, also does not see any faults in him. Neither of them thought about asking my wishes in this matter. My fate seems to be sealed as Rukmi has told Shishupala to come dressed as a bridegroom in just a few days. In the ceremony to be held before all, I will be given to him as his bride and life partner. O Lord, come and save your beloved Rukmini. Save me from the clutches of Shishupala before it is too late. Please tell the Brahmin who has carried my letter what your plan is and what I should do. He has cared for me all my life. You can tell him everything without hesitation. Rest assured that I will receive the message that you give him.

Till we meet,

Your beloved, Rukmini.'

On reading this letter Krishna was overwhelmed. He bowed down deeply to his visitor."Revered Brahmin," he said. "So you have always taken care of the Princess as if she were your own daughter?"

"No, Lord, I have always revered her as a Goddess," replied the Brahmin. "I see in her the divine Lakshmi and I bow down in front of her. The King had asked me to instruct her in our scriptures. During that time, I developed feelings of care and protection for her. She is divine in appearance. She belongs with you, Oh divine Krishna. She always tells the truth. Now that I have seen your real form, I know. You are Jagannath, the Lord of the World. All my doubts have vanished after seeing you. Tell me, O Lord, what can we do? There is no time to be lost."

"Faithful Brahmin, you have come all this way on your own two feet. How did you manage to cross the ocean for reaching Dwarka? Please tell me. "

"O Krishna, I must admit that your blessings were always with me. When I reached near the shore, I closed my eyes and said a short prayer. I prayed that, if I am meant to meet Lord Krishna, then he will surely find a way for me to cross this wide stretch of water. At that time, a little boy called me in his sweet voice. 'Brahmin, please step into this boat.' I opened my eyes and saw a little boy with a boat. But I am sure the boatman was you, my Lord, in the form of a child.

"When the boy reached the island, he secured the boat on the shore and directed me to the palace. I thanked the sweet child and started walking towards the palace gates. When I looked behind me to wave to him, I was surprised to find that there was no one there."

Krishna smiled. "You were right," he said. "It was me. But now tell me exactly where I can meet Princess Rukmini."

"Lord, to the north of the city of Vidarbha, there is a huge Shiva Mandir," began the Brahmin. "Next to it, there is a dense forest where you can safely hide your chariot. Tomorrow, in preparation for her marriage, the Princess, together with the other ladies, will come to the temple to offer her prayers to Lord Shiva. You must very quickly approach her, tell her your name and whisk her away in your chariot. The best route would be through the dense forest, as no one will be able to follow you through it. They will lose track of your movements."

"Tell Princess Rukmini that I will be there tomorrow. But I shall need a good horse on which to make our escape. And you should reach there today to make these preparations."

"How is that possible?" The Brahmin wrung his hands in despair. "It took me three days to reach here. The situation is hopeless. Princess Rukmini is doomed. I have failed her. Now, no one can save her."

"Revered Pundit, do not worry." Lord Krishna smiled. "My chariot will take you there in no time and then you can tell the Princess the plan and assure her that I will be there. Tell her to be ready for all eventualities."

Then Lord Krishna called for his charioteer Satyaki and told him to take their guest immediately to Vidarbha and the old Brahmin thanked Lord Krishna, bowed down in front of him, and took his leave. A few hours later, Satyaki was back with the news that their guest had reached Vidarbha. Then, Krishna went to enlist the help of his brother Balarama, who gave his full support and blessings. He said that, in his view, war was inevitable and he would prepare the army.

Next day, Krishna left for Vidarbha at dawn. Seeing the chariot of Krishna landing in the agreed place in the forest, the Brahmin came forward leading a powerful horse. He passed the reins to Krishna.

"I will go to meet the Princess at the Shiva Mandir," he told him. "You will know her by the bracelet of red threads she will be wearing on her left arm, the auspicious thread that brides wear on the day of their marriage."

Very soon, Krishna saw Rukmini approaching at the head of a procession of the ladies of the court. They were chanting mantras to Lord Shiva and some of them were also dancing with joy. Rukmini was wearing a glorious red bridal dress heavily ornamented in gold. Jewels sparkled around her neck and arms and she looked like a goddess. Krishna recognised her immediately and was instantly captivated. Deep within himself, his soul had remembered hers and, mounting the horse, he galloped furiously to meet the procession.

Seeing this strange man approaching, the ladies of the court were shocked and frightened. It was as if a lion had suddenly, with one leap, landed in front of a herd of deer. The stranger looked like a murderous robber dressed all in black, with a patch over one eye. The ladies started screaming for help and ran in all directions, trying to escape the looming danger. In the sudden confusion, no one thought of guarding the Princess.

Without slowing the huge horse's pace, Krishna bent down to take Rukmini's hand and lifted her in front of him. It was done so quickly that she had no time to think or even pretend to save herself. She looked helpless and her ladies thought that their princess was being abducted. In fact, she was very relieved and happy, as she had recognised Krishna. The horse carried the two of them to the forest where Krishna's chariot was waiting and then disappeared amongst the trees.

Only then did the ladies wake up as if from a dream. Immediately, they began to scream: "Help, help, a robber has kidnapped our beloved Princess. Save her somebody, please save her." They rushed to the palace to tell the King and Queen and soon the entire court was in an uproar. Many people came rushing to help and ran with the Queen and King to the Mandir to find out what exactly had happened and the direction in which the Princess had been taken. People who had witnessed the abduction pointed towards the forest. Reaching there, the King and Rukmi, his son, saw an unbelievable sight. They recognised Krishna, King of the Yadavs, racing away with their Rukmini towards his hidden chariot. The King's anger knew no bounds. "See, there is Krishna, he is the thief. Quickly, stop him. He is abducting our beloved daughter by force. He must not be allowed to escape."

Rukmini's brother Rukmi was also furious and, mounting his chariot, he summoned the Commander of the Army to pursue the escaping Krishna. "Attack the evil Yadav at once! Defeat and stop him with your arrows and save my sister."

In the forest, only slightly ahead of everyone else, Krishna and Rukmini had reached their chariot and Daruk, the charioteer, immediately set off at a furious speed towards Dwarka. Seeing that Krishna had no intention of releasing his sister, Rukmi took up his bow and arrow and pursued them, together with Shishupala, Rukmini's betrothed, who had arrived with his army. He was aghast to see to what levels his own uncle, Krishna, could descend to foil his carefully laid plans. He had considered Rukmini already as his Queen, since both his friend Rukmi, and her father King Bhishmak, had signalled their willingness for the marriage.

"Stop!" he bellowed at Krishna."Behave like a Kshatriya. Stand and fight instead of running away. For once, follow the normal rules of war instead of acting like the coward that you are. If you do not stop, we will attack your city of Dwarka and destroy it."

Rukmi and Shishupala were riding their chariots so fast that their army had been left far behind. The two of them went on attacking Krishna's chariot all the way. They failed because Daruk was such a skilful driver that he managed to avoid them and drove even faster than before. Soon, they reached the shore opposite Dwarka where unexpectedly a fully-armed Balarama was waiting on his chariot. Not only that, the entire army under his command was drawn up ready to face them and protect Krishna.

Balarama was known as a very brave warrior, whom everyone was afraid to engage in battle. Seeing that Krishna was under attack, he charged against Rukmi and, after an hour's fierce fighting, managed to kill him. With his friend dead, Shishupala lost his courage, realising that he could not face Balarama alone and fled from the battle field. He did not want to risk his life for the sake of a mere girl. If he managed to remain alive, he reasoned, he would find many others. He even decided not to return to Vidarbha and instead went shame-facedly back to his own Kingdom.

Balarama, however, drenched in blood after destroying Rukmi and in a towering rage, proceeded to Vidarbha where he called loudly for the King. Seeing the intimidating figure at his door, Bhishmak began to tremble. Afraid for his own life, he bowed down in front of Balarama. "Balarama, why are you so angry?" he quavered. "And why are you covered in blood?"

Balarama answered, "Your daughter, Rukmini, was very afraid of Shishupala and my brother Krishna has tried to help her. In answer, Rukmi, your son, took up his arms and wanted to kill my brother and start a war. I saw them when they reached the shore to do this dastardly deed. Seeing that they both were ready to attack, I engaged them in a fight. In this struggle, Rukmi, your son, was killed. When Shishupala saw that Rukmi had died, he ran away. Listen, if you wish to take revenge for your son, take up your arms. I am ready for it."

On hearing these words from Balarama, Bhishmak understood the gravity of the situation. He said, "Please, let me explain. It was the time of the marriage of Rukmini. Suddenly, we saw Krishna taking Rukmini away on his chariot. It was natural that Rukmi would take up his arms to defend his sister.

"We were not aware that Rukmini had called upon Krishna to come and help her escape from this marriage. However, she did tell us that she did not like Shishupala. As Rukmi was Shishupala's close friend, the arrangements for the marriage still went ahead. As Rukmini does not wish for this relationship herself, then my fighting with you will serve no purpose. Please Balarama, do not be angry with me. I have already lost my beloved son, let us stop this fight right here. My heart is torn in two. I do not blame my son, but he also did not know the entire truth. We all accept that in our society normally the girls chose their own life partner. Why should I be angry against you?" Saying these words Bhishmak's eyes filled up with tears.

Seeing the King's sorrow, Balarama calmed down and answered, "Bhishmak, you are a very good man. These events happened so suddenly that we could not take you in confidence. I am also very sorry about the tragic end of your son, Rukmi. When I accidently make someone else sad, than my inner self is full of regrets. It was very unfortunate that in all this turmoil, your son lost his life. Seeing Shishupala together with him, made my blood boil. You know that he was very near to Kansa, our hated uncle. My quick action was based on my earlier experiences. After that event, Jarasandha continued to attack us, time and again, till we were forced to leave Mathura for a safer place. I have no quarrel with you. Oh King, please leave your sorrows and come to Dwarka to give your daughter's hand to Krishna and bless them both."

On hearing these words from the mighty Balarama, Bhishmak was relieved and gave him his due honours. Then, he went to tell the Queen what had happened and both became sunk in deepest mourning for the passing away of their son. However, the knowledge of Krishna's forthcoming marriage with their daughter gave them joy and, after some time, when they had achieved some peace within themselves, Bhishmak accompanied Balarama to Dwarka to give his daughter to Krishna and remained there You dared to kidnap Vak?during the three days of wedding celebrations. Then, he invited Krishna to come together with Rukmini to Vidarbha to receive the Queen's blessings and more celebrations were held.

The people of Vidarbha were very happy. Rukmini's friends sang songs of joy and made merry at Krishna's cost. They told him that he had come as a robber to their city but now he was bound with bonds of love. Krishna smiled on hearing these friendly words and remembered how much fun he used to have with the Gopis in Vrindavan.

Rukmini also received a great welcome from the people of Dwarka who knew that she was in reality Lakshmi, the Goddess of Prosperity.With her presence, prosperity did indeed spread in the entire area. Harvests were plentiful, poverty vanished and the city became rich and powerful.

☆☆☆☆☆

How Indra was Forced to Depart the Earth - Conspiracy of the Forces of Evil[4]

When Kali, Lord of the Iron Age, was growing up, his Grandfather, Rishi Kanva thought it was time to take him to a Rishi so that he could pursue his studies. Rishi Kanva knew that his grandson was mischievous, loved to inflict pain on others and was not wise. Many a time he committed acts that were reprehensible. He did not have a good reputation amongst his close relatives and his uncle, Rishi Narad, thought he was definitely unsuited to studying the scriptures. But, Kanva loved his grandson and thought the world of him.

For this reason, Kanva decided to take him to the Ashram of his esteemed friend, the famous Rishi Gautam. Situated in a forest, his place was enormous with the capacity to house thousands of students. The brightest student studying there was the first among the Gods, none other than Lord Indra himself. Together with his illustrious sons, Rishi Gautam imparted to the students their deep knowledge of the ancient scriptures, the Vedas, and the hidden secret behind various sounds

[4]Devayan Vol. 1/Brahma Kalpa/Pragatha Mandal/Durvidya Varga/ Chapter 1-5/pages 917-954

and words, together with their spiritual significance. There were separate classes organised for Gods, for Rishis, as well as, for human beings. Kali, being born in a Rishi family, was eminently suitable.

However, as soon as any lesson began, whether on the hidden significance of sounds or on the laws governing creation, Kali felt so sleepy that all his efforts were concentrated on keeping his eyes open. Finally, he went shamefacedly to his teachers and told them about his difficulty and they in turn asked Indra for help.

Indra realised that this sudden sleep could not be normal. Usually, the atmosphere in such an Ashram was very pure and remained without any outside disturbances. So, he thought, that it must somehow be coming from negative forces either outside the periphery of the Ashram or somewhere very near. He decided to stand on guard in front of the room where Kali was receiving his instruction and soon found out that his suspicions were correct. He discovered that it was Shani, Adharma himself, who was lurking outside the room. It was he, who had been influencing Kali with sleep and ignorance, precisely at the time when the lessons started.

Indra understood that Shani did not want Kali to learn the secret wisdom of the Vedas and the Upanishads, and the great significance that the sounds and words carried in them. Shani wanted Kali to remain ignorant of this highest knowledge. In fact, his eventual aim was that Kali should be the one to drive out all knowledge and spirituality from the world. However, once Indra began guarding the room where the instruction was being given, Shani's power could not reach Kali, who could then understand his lessons without any difficulty.

Seeing all his efforts fail, Shani went to see his Guru, Shukracharya, and together they decided that the only solution was to remove Indra from Rishi Gautam's Ashram with the help of three powerful dark forces acting in unison: Dwandwa, the spirit of discord, Nakta, the deep darkness of midnight and Sandhya, the dusk of the evening.

The plan was simple. Shani should be present at the time when Rishi Gautam was giving lessons to Indra on the Universal Law of Creation, the eternal Dharma that exists above all of creation. By bringing negative forces into the area, confusion, discord and doubt would be sown in the minds of both the teacher and the student and, as a result, conflict between them would arise in such a way that Indra would be accused, insulted and driven away from the Ashram.

Shani, however, was still worried. "Guruji, Indra is all powerful," he said. "If he has even an inkling of my presence as well as of the negative forces there, he is quite able to resist all our attempts."

Shukracharya reassured him. "Do not worry, Shani, I will be there together with Sandhya. There is so much influence and power at my command that you should have no doubts. But, please go and tell Nakta and Sandhya to come here also."

When Shani entered the place where Nakta was, he was received with great respect. Bowing down before him he said: "Please tell me, O Shani, what you want of me. I am always at your service."

"Nakta, I want you to accompany me to Rishi Gautam's Ashram," Shani replied. "You must remember that a portion of your own self, was instrumental in bringing Kali into the mortal world. Your help was absolutely essential in this major task. Kali was born in Rishi Kanva's family as the son of Pragatha and Gathini. Now, he is studying in Rishi Gautam's Ashram. You remember, I had received blessings from Mahamaya that my policies would be promoted by Kali, when he becomes the Leader of the new Age. In fact, he would be so powerful that the Age would be named after him and be called the Kali Yuga.

"Please come with me now to Rishi's Gautam's Ashram. We have to take action so that the Day of the Gods, the Golden Age, is brought to a sudden and cataclysmic end. Nakta, you are very powerful,but you will still have to join hands with Sandhya, who controls the forces of darkness. Both of you, together with Vibhavari, the power of sleep, please come to the Ashram."

Hearing this message from Shani, Nakta was beside himself with joy. Finally, his time had come. He rubbed his hands with satisfaction. Now, he could exert his own powers in the world, spread his influence all around and create mischief. "O Son of Surya, the Sun God," he replied. "I am greatly honoured that you have manifested in this form in front of me. Please tell me what the situation in the Ashram is? And how will the forces of darkness and sleep affect it?"

"Listen carefully to me" answered Shani. "I have been asked by our great Teacher, Shukracharya, to seek your help. The four-armed Kali, Rishi Kanva's grandson, has come to the Ashram for his education. As he is from the family of Rishis, his Teacher is Nodha, the son of Rishi Gautam. Nodha is giving him the knowledge of Varna and Upanishads. At the same time, he is treating me with contempt. How dare he provide knowledge to Kali? You know very well that, Kali's birth was brought about by us all to promote the Age of Darkness, of Falsehood. How can we allow Kali to take any path other than that of Adharma? How can we allow him to gain this universal knowledge and become wise? If Kali starts to promote harmony and Dharma in this world, then all that we have done until now would be in vain. Imagine, even in his Age, we will have no place in the Universe. I have been living all this time in Naraka, the deepest Hell, where the Sun shines not. It is pitch black there at all times. I am not even allowed to come to the other worlds. I have no power at all.

"For this reason, I have come to you now as Rishi Gautam and Lord Indra are presently discussing the intricacies of universal law. Shukracharya, my Guru, intends to unleash his powerful forces to promote conflict in that atmosphere. When this quarrel and disharmony escalates, you are to spread your force of darkness in the Ashram. With all these powers swirling around them, the discussion between the Guru and the Student will become heated and full of discord. We intend that as a result of this engineered quarrel, Indra should be thrown out of the Ashram.

"Be careful however," warned Shani. "For you will have to exert your influence cleverly on Indra without his becoming aware of the fact that an outside force is influencing him. Make him feel drowsy for he has the power to ward off any outside attack if he comes to know of it. If anything more is needed, I will let you know. The main purpose of our combined efforts is to remove Indra from his position as the Leader of the Gods and to destroy the power of the Rishis."

Immediately after this visit, Shani made his way to Rishi Gautam's Ashram, followed closely by Nakta, the spirit of darkness. There, he found Rishi Gautam in an intense discussion with his favourite pupil, Indra. Having explained his own position, he invited Indra to express his views.

"I do have some reservations in this position," Indra began. "Guruji, you said that all women of the world, who are not part of one's family, should be regarded as mothers, that one should see only the mother in another woman. But, how exactly can this be true? Since it is normal that everyone marries a girl outside the family, then how can one marry someone if they regard her as their own mother?

"When a husband enters into the womb of a woman in the form of a seed and a child is created, after that the husband cannot address his wife as his Mother. Again, a child's way of looking at a mother is different than when a young man looks at a woman. Please tell me: when a man is attracted towards a woman, how does the love for a mother come into it. We need to have a strict law on this so that everyone can follow it without having any doubts. So, please guide me, Guruji, which is the right way? The boundaries between these two are not very clear. If wrong emotions spread all over the world then Dharma will be polluted. We have to remove this confusion from men's mind and heart. If you can give me clear guidance in this respect then I can spread it to the whole world.

"Intelligent persons look at their own wives as Mothers," Rishi Gautam replied calmly. "Just as the life partner of a Guru is regarded as Mother by the students. When a young girl gives birth to children she takes the role of a Mother. If the man still looks at her as a woman and the feeling of desire enters into the relationship then her image is distorted."

At this point Dwandwa, the spirit of conflict, entered secretly into the atmosphere in the room. Neither Rishi Gautam nor Lord Indra were aware of this fact, but they started become increasingly conscious of differences between them, each feeling that theirs was the correct standpoint. They even began to get angry.

"Indra, listen," said Rishi Gautam, "I am telling you that everyone should look at all the women of the world as their mother. We should not confuse ourselves with how the Gods regard women and how human beings look at them. You should not think like human beings. If you contest this view, then Indra, I feel that you are revealing to me that you have an argumentative nature."

"Guruji,why are you so angry?" asked Indra. "I am just explaining my viewpoint and answering your questions. You seem to be very confused yourself. Please think about this problem peacefully and give me your answer."

Then Gautam Rishi exploded with anger and hurt. His own favourite student answering him with so with so much impudence was more than he could bear. "How dare you tell your own Guru that his mind is confused," he said. "You are forgetting yourself."

"We are discussing this question," replied Indra. "In reply to your suggestion, I am merely giving you my view." Indra had spoken calmly, but suddenly, he too felt Shukra's power and, without knowing why, he was filled with rage and his body started to burn and tremble. "You tell me that I am muddled. I think that you are confused about universal law and justice and that's why you are getting so angry without giving me a proper answer."

Rishi Gautam became angrier still. "Such behaviour is far beyond what is allowed in my Ashram. I would suggest that you go back home to the heavens. You need no more instructions from me. Your mind is concentrating its energy only in sensual enjoyment and physical desires. You do not know what it means to renounce your desires. You are filled with stupidity and ignorance. In the heavens, you can make your own laws and you don't need my help."

Indra was crushed. Without saying a word, he bowed down before his revered Guru, touched his feet and left the room, determined to return home to the high heavens. Rishi Gautam was still so angry that he made no attempt to stop him. Then Sandhya, the evening dusk, spread her darkness all over the Ashram which, being spiritual, as well as physical, created an atmosphere of hopeless sorrow amongst all the inhabitants.

Indra was also influenced by this insidious feeling. He went straight to a deep dark forest, where no one could disturb him. Consumed with sadness at leaving the Ashram, he could not understand why suddenly everything had gone so wrong. Meanwhile, Nakta, the essence of darkness and Tamas that of ignorance, began to infiltrate the Ashram. Rishi Gautam was beginning to wonder what would happen if the Leader of the Gods left the Ashram in such a manner. Surely, it would cause great problems in heaven and on earth. He needed to discuss what was to be done with his consort Ahalya, a very wise woman, and his learned sons who were also highly realised souls. But, first, it was time for his evening dip in the river Gomati, which flowed by the Ashram.

Kali was observing all that was happening in the Ashram when he saw Shani approaching. With deep respect, he stood still and waited for him to come near.

"The time has come for you to perform your duty,' Shani told him. "Go to Gautami immediately and tell her about the conflict between Indra and Rishi Gautam. Tell her that her husband ordered Indra to leave the Ashram and then come back to me."

Kali hurried to do exactly as Shani had instructed and told Gautami how disrespectfully Indra had acted towards the Rishi. Of course she, like everyone else in the Ashram, was under the influence of Nakta's negative force. Still her first thought was how to prevent Indra from leaving the Ashram. Not stopping to see whether her hair and her clothes were in order, she asked Kali if he knew where Indra was.

"I saw him going towards the forest at the other end of the Ashram, Mother," Kali answered. "It is very far from here."

Gautami immediately started running further into the deep forest. She looked neither to right or left, thinking only of finding Indra. Evening was advancing and it was fast becoming darker as Sandhya cast a shadow around her before reporting back to Shani.

Meanwhile, Shani was very happy to hear about the disturbances occurring in the Ashram. "Come, Sandhya," he said. "Our plans are moving quickly and soon we will reach our goal. Let's go and hear what Ahalya says to Indra."

Indra saw Gautami rushing towards him from a distance and was worried to see her coming alone to the forest. He stood and bowed down in front of her. "Why did you come here, Mother? Has anything happened to you? I must tell you that earlier I had a confrontation with the revered Rishi and he ordered me to leave the Ashram immediately. So, I am going to return to the heavens."

Ahalya was shocked. "Son, you are an important part of the Ashram. You should not think of leaving us in such haste. Go and talk once again with the Guru."

"I respect you very highly," Indra apologised. "But I have to do as my Guru told me. Please give me your blessings so that I can proceed to heaven."

Ahalya was deeply moved. "I still think you should finish your studies," she told him. "And only then think of going home."

Then, Indra told her what had actually happened in the lessons that day. "During a discussion on Universal Law, I had differences with my esteemed Guru. When there are differences, these could then lead to conflicts."

"I do not know what differences you have with your Guru," replied Ahalya. "But I tell you that if you modify your position in the discussion, then your Guru will also change his views. Otherwise, you can accept his views and make them your own. This should not be so difficult."

The calm reasoning of Gautami started to influence Indra. He was willing to accept her advice. But Sandhya was nearby and, seeing that Ahalya was about to ruin their plans and restore peace and harmony to the Ashram, she rushed to tell Shani.

Desperate situations required intense efforts. "Kali," Shani turned to him. "Go immediately to the banks of the river Gomati where Rishi Gautam is taking his evening bath. Tell him to come and observe Indra and Gautami. Tell him how strange it is that Indra and Gautami are meeting each other in such a deserted part of the forest."

Kali rubbed his hands with glee. He was thrilled to see that with just a couple of well-placed words, he would be able to plant doubt in the great Rishi's mind. He loved to create mischief, and he was tired of presenting himself as a good being. It was so boring. He hurried to the river bank.

"Guruji, please come quickly," he called out to Gautam. "Wicked Indra is taking away your Gautami, our Mother. They have both gone to the dense forest at the outskirts of the Ashram."

Rishi Gautam was outraged. He came immediately out of the river and, still in his wet clothes, rushed to the forest.

Gautami was still telling Indra that he should let go of his anger and go back to his Guru. She held his hands in hers as she tried to convince him. "A Guru is always to be worshipped. Your Guru is elderly and is always correct. If a Guru is angry with the student, then it is good for him. It is very wrong if the student is angry with his Guru."

Rishi Gautam saw all this from a distance. He observed also that his wife was not properly dressed and her hair was dishevelled, when usually in public she was very dignified and her clothes were also formal. Being too far away to hear what she was saying, he completely misunderstood that was happening and rushed towards them shouting loudly. This so shocked and startled Indra and Gautami that they became like statues, unable to move.

Indra had earlier wanted to apologise to his Guru for the heated words exchanged before and to ask him for forgiveness but when he saw the Rishi's furious face, he was frozen with fear. The Rishi's eyes were emitting sparks of fire which began to scorch Indra's skin and he felt sure that they were on the brink of some disaster. When Gautam started to speak it seemed as if the earth and the sky and all the beings in between must have also felt that something dire was going to happen.

"Gautami, tell me why have you come to meet Indra in this secluded place?" Gautam thundered. "Why are you here in this deep forest so far away from home? You have surely sinned. Indra is like a son to you. But the fact remains, that he is not your son."

Gautami was dumbfounded. She thought her husband had lost his mind and hastened to explain. "Indra had decided to go to heaven without taking leave from me," she said. "I came to him to tell him not to go away without finishing his studies."

But Rishi Gautam was too angry to hear what she said. His mind and his thoughts being darkened by both, Shukra and Kali, he was unable to hear what was being said. "Just look at yourself, Gautami," he said again. "You have made yourself beautiful and attractive for meeting someone else. You have a husband and sons at home. But you pay no attention to your husband, your sons and even your home. Instead, you look at Indra with lust in your eyes. You have a heart of stone and so you will remain like a stone. You will become a statue of stone and you will remain here in this deserted place for aeons to come."

Then Rishi Gautam turned to Indra. "Indra, you are stupid. Look at the light coming out of my eyes. You dared to touch my wife in this deserted place with lust in your mind. She is like a Mother to you. She is my consort. How should I mete out justice to you? You are going against the laws of right conduct. I curse you, that as your mind is full of desires, your body should demonstrate to all and sundry, to what level you have sunk. All over your body you will have the signs of your hidden desire made manifest to the entire world."

Such was Gautam's power that these curses had an immediate impact. Indra looked down at his body and, to his horror; he could see innumerable images of a woman's genitals marked vividly all over his body. Not only that, this curse destroyed his divine light and made it weak and dim. Seeing the beautiful body of Indra becoming so dull, the Rishi started feeling ashamed of his act. He started questioning himself whether he had acted wisely. He began to tremble as he thought of what he had done.

But Indra simply replied: "Guruji, what you have said must be the truth. Who am I to feel any sorrow or disappointment? Everything is your blessing. Please give me your permission to depart now. My time here has come to an end." Saying this, he covered himself completely from head to toe in dark clothing so that no one could observe the signs of shame that were covering his body.

"Oh Devendra, please, do not leave from here; please stay," Rishi Gautam pleaded. "A problem has arisen. Let us solve it together." But Indra did not listen to him and continued to walk away.

Now Gautam began to realise the full horror of what he had done. If the Leader of the Gods was cursed, how could he administer the heavens? How could he himself hold *yajnas*, when Indra could not receive the offerings that would bring results? If he hid himself from sight, then how would he be able to carry his fearful weapon, the Vajra? Without it, the demons would be able to control the heavens and the earth.

There was no one in the world who could replace Indra, none who could manage the affairs of the heavens, neither Chandra, nor Agni, nor Surya nor Brihaspati. No one had his power and his bravery. Vishnu remained always silently occupied in his yogic sleep. Who would face the obstacles that come in the way of creation, who would remove them? Neither Rudra, nor Brahma, nor Marut, nor Varuna, the Leader of the Oceans, had the power and the gift of winning all the battles. If there is no one to protect the heavens, divine power will weaken and then who will protect the world from all its sorrows and sufferings? Who will bring peace to the world and maintain unity?

With his mind battling to understand all the consequences, Gautam saw from a distance Nakta, Kali and Shani huddled in a dark corner of the Ashram and could even hear their conversation.

"Look Shani," Shukra was saying, "you can destroy the entire Ashram where knowledge resided, tarnish the pride and fame of the heavens and banish Truth from creation. See, Indra is now, at this very moment, leaving the world and even the entire creation. Now, the right time has come. Please establish Kali firmly as the Leader of the Age. Together with Kali, you and Shani should administer the entire world and overturn Dharma."

Hearing these words from his Guru, Kali was overjoyed and the three of them jubilantly left the Ashram on their various errands. With them, went their evil influence in the Ashram and Rishi Gautam regained his former intelligence and judgement.

Silently Gautam spoke to Indra. "O Indra, you can never do any injustice, any evil act. I cursed you for no reason. Bear this curse for some time and hide yourself. It is the evil Time that has influenced us. Now, Truth will leave Creation and the evil time will start. My actions were done under a cloud of doubt."

Then he had an idea. He decided to go immediately to consult Brahma. But as he was leaving the Ashram, he heard Ahalya's voice coming like a whisper from the statue that she had become.

"O Lord, you gave me a curse under the influence of your anger. Before leaving, please tell me when I will be released from it."

Hearing her plea Gautam sat down and went into a deep meditation for several hours. When he opened his eyes he had already received knowledge from within. He addressed Gautami.

"Listen Ahalya, I have come to know the truth. Neither Indra, the Leader of the Gods, nor you were guilty of any sin. All these misunderstandings occurred because I allowed myself to become angry and let rage control me. It was my fault. Now listen to me carefully. You know that Kali was brought to the Ashram by the wise Rishi Kanva. However, he has remained all the time here under the influence of Shukracharya, Nakta and Shani who all incited him to do evil. Now he, Kali, the future Leader of the Age, the infamous Kaliyuga, will be able to take control of creation and Indra will lose his glory in the heavens. The influence of heaven on earth will vanish. This will have a calamitous impact on creation.

"All good will vanish from the world - belief in the Gods, the influence of Rishis on the world, truth and justice. Instead, Adharma will spread its influence in the entire world. Law and justice will disappear under Shukracharya. I had not known before that they all were active here."

On hearing this explanation from the Brahmrishi, Gautami was distraught. Instead of thinking about her own pain, she reflected sadly on what the world would have to endure. Tears streamed from her eyes and for a little time she remained quiet with her head bowed down. Then she spoke, her voice filled with sorrow, "Please tell me more about how the world will suffer under Adharma. Indra is cursed and he has left the heavens. Who will then protect this creation, which power will save it from the pain given by Adharma? I find this situation the most painful. What is my suffering if the world is going to go through all these calamities?"

Gautam Rishi answered, "What I saw when I meditated was that Kali will not be able to exercise his full powers for some time still. To stop his nefarious plans against the Lord of Truth, the brave sons of Rishi Aptya will be very effective. A tremendous conflict and struggle will start between Kali and these two sons, Trita and Dwita. They will remain active for some time, Ahalya. But still this evil time will eventually prevail. Its destructive influence will be further strengthened by Nakta, Shani and Shukra. Now the Rakshasas and the Panis will gain strength. After some time, Indra will become free from the curse that I unfortunately and unknowingly gave him. But his strength and power will be significantly diminished. Due to this, he will not be able to conquer these adverse forces.

"As a consequence, the Asuras will gain power in Heaven and the Gods will be serving them. Seeing this condition of the Gods, Brahma will ask Bhuvan to make efforts to awaken Vishnu from his deep yoga induced meditation. As a result, he will take birth in a human shape as Sri Rama on this world to destroy the Asuras and to re-establish the Gods in the heavens. At that time, Ahalya, you will be redeemed and, together with Rama, return to live in the Ashram."

Rishi Gautam set off from the Ashram and as he went he heard these words from Ahalya's statue: "How long will you roam in the forests? Our sons are restless, they have no peace and they will go on wandering around me and because of this I fear the entire Ashram will be destroyed."

And that is precisely what happened. All the work done in the Ashram, the tuition given to the students, the discussions on important issues, came to a sudden stop. Ahalya had to witness every last person leaving the Ashram until the whole area was deserted and she was left alone in that deep forest.

☆☆☆☆☆

Homer-Divine Messenger of Truth[5]

The Immortals had gone from the earth. They had tried to spread the message of divine love in the mortal world during the Kali Yuga but it had become completely distorted through the impact of Kali and his negative cohorts. Still, wishing to help humanity during these dire times they went to meet Rishi Vyasa in the higher worlds to obtain his advice.

The great poet was very worried to hear about what was happening in the world. He turned towards Vibhishan. "Remember the Lanka where you were born? It is surrounded by a great ocean and is situated at the south of Bharat. West of there is where the demons under Ravan fled to save themselves. But they never gave up their desire for power, in fact, that wish has grown even more intense; and now, once more, they are eyeing the great land of Bharat. If they manage to come to India, they will have a terrible impact on its culture and the Sanatana Dharma, the eternal religion, and their influence will plague India for centuries to come.

"To avert this catastrophe, we will have to take certain steps. We have to remember that this country,

[5]Devayan Vol. 9/Rudra Kalpa/Arbuda Mandal/Darshaka Varga/Chapter 9-11/ pages 1446-1452

Bharat, is the chosen one where the Gods and Rishis come again and again. They always live here and it is only from here that the divine influence will spread again. Someone will have to go down to the world again to prevent and delay this calamity, if possible. What do you think?"

The Immortals were relieved to see a glimmer of hope in this dire situation. "We can call upon your wise disciple, Sanjay," they suggested. "You remember how, being able to see events from a great distance, he kept the blind King Dhritrashtra informed of all happenings during the Great War in Kurukshetra."

Rishi Vyasa then called Sanjay. "Sanjay, you must go to the mortal world again and take birth. This will be to undertake a great mission. In your new birth, you will have to take your inherent wisdom and the knowledge of the Puranas together with you. You can decide yourself where you wish to take birth, but I would like to suggest the country called Greece where there lives a great family called Harm. You should take birth there and your name will then be Homer."

During the time of Kali, Gods and Rishis were not allowed to come down to the earth to take birth and the evil Time Lord was furious to hear that Sanjay was daring to commit this crime. He immediately called upon Arbuda, King of the Serpents. "Follow Sanjay at all times," he said. "He is powerful and will hinder our efforts to bring the entire world under our control."

Arbuda saw that Sanjay was heading towards the family of Harm to take birth and he, himself, took up a position nearby. When Harm's wife was asleep he entered her womb and to his surprise, found Sanjay already established there. Sanjay recognised the intruder immediately and there began a huge battle for supremacy between the two forces. Harm's wife awoke in great pain and, not knowing the cause, was very scared. Sanjay soon managed to burn Arbuda so badly that the King of the Serpents was forced to leave her womb to save himself, but not before he had destroyed Sanjay's eyes with his deadly poison.

Homer was born completely blind but he possessed a great inner knowledge, and the strength of his soul increased day by day. He had acute hearing and a perfect memory so that whatever he heard, he remembered. Even when he was an infant he amazed his neighbours and friends by speaking in verse and everyone loved him. As he grew older, his poetic skills continued to improve and his fame spread far and wide. People often wondered: how can a blind person who had never seen the world, never experienced the brightness of sunshine, the glory of moonlight, the green grass, the colourful flowers, how can he describe it all so beautifully and powerfully? They were spell bound.

When they asked Homer how he managed to write poetry and to describe everything so well, he answered that he had inner eyes, inner knowledge. He said that real knowledge lies in the power of the mind to visualize. The eyes that we all have are just instruments for this vital experience; without the help of the mind, we cannot make sense of all that we see.

This house, this entire area, this huge tree with its myriads of branches, the singing birds, the colours of the flowers, the animals, the clarity of the water falling from the mountain above and forming the impressive waterfall are all understood by the mind. The Sun, the Moon, the stars above, the clouds, the lightning, the planets, the storm, the rain, we grasp this reality around us only through the mind. Our knowledge, past and present, helps us see the world around us.

A very small child on seeing an object, asks his mother what it is and stores her reply in his mind so that the next time, when he sees the same, he knows what that object is without asking his mother. When knowledge is gained through yogic austerities then the vision is vast and meaningful. With inner knowledge, one can see the world very clearly and understand all the complex situations without any hindrances and barriers.

Crowds gathered by Homer's house every day to learn more. Many visited him to ask his advice about the problems they were facing. They asked him about birth and death, about health and diseases, about happiness and sufferings. They questioned him about how the child enters into the womb of the mother, and how his body develops. They also wondered why only certain wombs could bear a child and others not. They asked him why all ailments vanished when death came. What happened to the body when one slept, and how did one become conscious the moment one woke up? What happened when consciousness left the body, where did it go? Which religion does the departed soul choose? What thoughts does it have, and how and when does it again take birth?

People also asked Homer to tell them more about Lord Indra, the Leader of the Gods, and about the work of Chandra, the Moon God. What are the areas of work of the Sun, the Wind, the Fire, and what are their different powers? Who is the Creator of all the beings in this world, where is this God? Homer answered every question in great detail and in verse and metre using his knowledge of the Puranas of India. He told them that all human beings come to the mortal world with this inherent knowledge but that undivine forces also influence life and create obstacles.

Homer's listeners were filled with joy and revered and praised him. The local rulers provided him with all that he needed to help him lead a comfortable life. He ensured that his teachings were saved for posterity through written epics before leaving his mortal body and the world and returning to the Immortals as Sanjay. But many people thereafter remembered his lessons and, becoming more philosophical, realised that life is not all about seeking enjoyment and acquiring money and power. A simple life can bring as much happiness and contentment.

☆☆☆☆☆

Return of Indra–The Yajna of the Balkhilya Rishis[6]

Satyadeva, the God of Truth, reigned in the heavens but on the earth the negative powers of old age, disease, death, anger, fear and greed still ruled supreme. Satyadeva could see that that no force on earth could either eradicate or provide any relief from them. They had made human life a journey of misery, pain and despair and the Golden Age could not descend in such an atmosphere. Truth had to be experienced by each and every human being on earth. But how could it be brought about? It was a mammoth task, a task that only a God could perform.

Now, Indra was considered to be the most powerful God. Not only was he the Leader of the Gods, but he also had thousands of eyes, so that he could observe all happenings in the universe at any given moment. Nothing big or small escaped his attention and he was also respected by all and the Gods bowed down in front of him. In order to prepare for the coming of the Golden Age, it was he who had to be persuaded to descend to the earth and take birth as a human being. For this, a *yajna*, a great sacrifice, had to be held.

[6]Devayan Vol. XI/Indra Mandala/Balkhilya Varga/ Chapter 1–6/pages 3773-3785

The Creator, Brahma, turned to the Balkhilya Rishis. These nine sons of Kanva Rishi, one of the seven Rishis who came from the mind of Brahma, had attained the ultimate knowledge very early in their life. After that, they had stopped growing physically and still looked and sounded like young boys. But, they were extremely powerful.

They were highly realised souls, and were famous for their intense austerities. They knew all about Creation, about Brahma and were known authorities on the Vedas. All their lives had been spent in holding *yajnas*, ceremonial sacrifices, mainly for the benefit of the world. Completely liberated, they were free of any attachment to the mortal world, had never wanted to be married, and thus had no additional responsibilities. So, these boy Rishis were given the task of invoking Indra and entreating him to take a mortal birth.

Immediately, they started to make their preparations. First of all, they had to decide where the sacrificial fire would be lit. Then they had to gather sufficient wood and ghee without knowing how long the fire would have to burn before they would be successful. Finally, they took their places around the sacrificial fire as the priests at this great ceremony. The eldest of the Rishis, Praskanva, took upon himself the important task of ladling ghee in the fire and they all began to chant the powerful Vedic mantras that would force Indra to come down to earth.

Indra, always attentive, though far away in the highest heavens, became conscious of this strange activity on the lower plane. When he heard the chanting of the mantras, he paid more attention in order to discover the purpose for which this ceremony was being held. He soon recognised the serious significance of these particular mantras but could not understand why these were being chanted in children's voices. He knew that usually only well-known Rishis, with sonorous voices, conducted such important *yajnas* and decided that it must be only some boys playing, practicing at holding a *yajna*. But still he was curious.

Indra soon understood that the boys were trying to force him, the all-powerful Leader of the Gods, to come down to the earth, to bring in the Golden Age. Usually, even when only one God was called, a huge sacrificial ceremony was organised. But to summon Lord Indra, the Leader of the Gods, it was as if to call upon all the Gods. Such ceremonies should therefore be even more magnificent, on a very large scale, with the sacrificial flames rising high into the sky.

Now, the entire area for this ceremony was only a few feet and the sacrificial fire was tiny. Even the utensils for the ghee were really small and the spoons used to ladle the ghee in the fire could hold only a little amount. It all seemed ridiculous to Indra. To call him down upon the earth, away from his many duties, and for so great a task as the changing of the Age, was in no way a child's play. In fact, he found it hilarious and could not control his laughter and when the other Gods saw Indra laughing at the puny efforts of the Balkhilya Rishis, they also began to laugh.

When the Rishis saw that the Gods were laughing at them, they were furious. They did not like being made fun of. But they did not allow their emotions to disturb them and continued their sacrificial ceremony.

However, this fury began to build up within them and very soon had produced such a great heat that it started to stream out from their bodies with an ever-increasing intensity. The temperature also began to rise. Soon, even the Gods began to feel the effects of the heat while the Balkhilyas continued relentlessly with their *yajna*.

Now Lord Indra was really worried. He could also feel the intense power coming from the efforts made by those small Rishis. When even the heavens, that normally were protected, began to burn; the other Gods begged him to do something. Lord Indra called urgently upon the clouds and the Rain God, Parjanya, to come and relieve his own agony and that of the other Gods and to cool down and save the creation.

The clouds came rushing in from all directions with a huge clamour. There were loud bursts of thunder and streaks of lightning from one end of the sky to the other. It became very dark with only lightning bolts piercing the gloom and then the clouds began to burst, heavy rain poured down and all areas became flooded.

When there was no dry spot left in the entire Creation, even the sacrificial fire of the boy Rishis was extinguished, and the Balkhilyas also found themselves in danger of being drowned. To save themselves from the torrential rain they swam to a huge tree and hid under some enormous leaves. But the anger within them went on increasing and again built up such a heat that the flood turned into steam and dried up. The clouds began to lose their water and started vanishing; and the Balkhilya Rishis were able to find a dry place, re-light their sacrificial fire and renew their chanting.

Now that the laughter had stopped, the tiny Rishis no longer felt angry. With all their powers concentrated on the ceremony, Indra experienced its full force. To his dismay, he felt himself being pulled, together with his charioteer, directly towards the *yajna* but, though he came near the earth, he remained whirling around in the sky.

Then, Rishi Praskanva spoke to him. "Hear me, O Indra," he said. "It is Satyadeva himself, the son of Rishi Abhivarta, who is the driving force behind this *yajna.* Please enter into the sacrificial fire without delay. You are the one who has accomplished hundreds of impossible tasks. You are the one who defeated Vritra. Oh immense Indra, listen to me and come to take a mortal birth to commence the Golden Age."

The Balkhilyas all joined in their brother's prayers. "O Indra, bring the Gods down into the mortal plane but retain your divine qualities, even when you exist as a human being. Remember, Indra that in this immense human world there is, at present, no belief in Gods. We beg you to re-establish it once again in mankind."

The Balkhilyas continued to implore Indra to enter into the sacrificial fire until at last, Indra himself took a miniscule form and entered into the holy fire which immediately gained in strength and reached up to the heavens, uniting them with the earth. The Balkhilyas then brought the *Yajna* to a halt and the Gods bowed down and honoured them. No-one now noticed the Rishis' size; they only wondered at and admired their incredible strength. All were overjoyed that the Golden Age was soon to begin, for with the coming of the new

Age, in daily life, the good will reign supreme and evil will be banished.

☆☆☆☆☆

Kali Fights Back–Strategy to Delay the Golden Age[7]

To end the evil perpetrated in the mortal world by Kali, Lord of the Iron Age, the Creator ordered him to remain in mid-space until the Gods and Rishis arrived to announce the Golden Age. When Kali heard the Gods loudly celebrating the birth of Truth in the higher world, he was enraged. He knew that, being far from the world, there was nothing he could do to prevent the beginning of his own descent into the netherworlds. But, then he remembered his old ally Arbuda, the King of the Snakes, and called to him.

Arbuda, with his myriad heads, had been busy following Kali's instructions to keep on misleading the world, promoting evil activities and dark ignorance. One of his successes was to infuse his vital energy into material nature, thereby creating electricity. As a result, humanity became involved in discovering its benefits as technology developed bringing great material progress. With the next invention, the telephone, people obtained the awe-inspiring gift of being able to hear voices over long distances. Later on, as we know, there

---

[7]Devayan/Vol. 10/Rudra Kalpa/UdyamMandala/Sanveda Varga/Chapter 7-10/pages 2883-2891

came radio and television, whereby one could even see pictures of events happening in far off places.

Everyone welcomed these new achievements, not knowing that in the Golden Age the human senses of vision and hearing will so expand that such abilities will become second nature without the need for instruments. Instead, people put their efforts into making new inventions and achieving material well-being and paid no attention to their spiritual development or nurturing divine values in their lives.

When Arbuda heard Kali calling him he thought that the Leader of the Age wanted to congratulate him on all his praiseworthy achievements. He was sure that Kali would be happy to hear all that he had done in his absence. Delegating all his powers to his capable and powerful sons, he asked them to continue to carry out his work while he was away. But when he arrived and offered his greetings to his Lord, he was surprised to see that Kali was extremely angry. His three eyes burned with wrath as he told Arbuda of his banishment to mid-space.

"You know already, Arbuda, that the Creator had gone down to the world as a mere mortal being, his purpose being to facilitate the descent of the Gods there and to begin the Golden Age. He forced me to remain here to ensure that the manifestation of Truth is accomplished without any obstruction. Since that time, I have been here, waiting till he comes back and decides what to do with me.

"I did not try to defend myself for it is true that I have always worked against the Gods and, looking down upon the world, I could see that he was right. The entire world was really following my anti-divine policies. Then, he told me I shall be marooned here until Satyadeva, the Lord of Truth, descends to the mortal world with the divine army of Gods. I must pay my respects, welcome and guide them so that they do not waste any time in achieving their goal. He added that I should remember that I was born in the family of Rishis and now that my time in the world has come to an end, I should help the Rishis and the Gods when their Age is coming.

"So Arbuda, I have called you here to tell you what your role will be while I am stuck here. Listen carefully. This celebration in the higher worlds is the beginning of the Golden Age, where both the Gods and the Rishis will be fully active. You can hear the Gandharvas singing and the Apsaras dancing to welcome the coming Age. During my Age, I had put them into a deep sleep of ignorance, in which they became completely unconscious. Now, through the efforts of the Rishis, the Gods have also woken up and all of them are ready for action. However, for us, there is some time left, about two hundred years, before Usha, the Divine Dawn, comes down to the mortal world."

Arbuda was very happy to hear that he could still do something to spread Kali's dark shadow over the world. "Tell me, O Lord of the Iron Age, what I should do. I am always your servant. No one in this world adores you more than me."

Kali replied: "Create hindrances and obstacles to delay the advent of the Golden Age. Obstruct the divine with your lower vital forces of anger, greed, chaos and lies. At all times, cast a distorting and threatening shadow on the consciousness of mortal beings so that they cannot see the difference between positive and negative forces. Let no beam of divine light reach them. Blanket the world with ignorance in such a way that humans remain unaware of the effervescent joy in the higher worlds. Make them unconscious of their inherent divine nature and increase their disbelief in Gods. Such a viewpoint should be considered modern, attractive and rational.

"Tell them that the divine epics are just powerful words: a poet's imagination, they are not something that really happened. Teach them that they should stop pining for the Gods and focus on taking action. Promote only those epic poems that describe nature and those that provide happiness and joy. Let people concentrate on them and enjoy them. Real knowledge will thus be side-lined and forgotten. Tell them that joy is possible only from material things, from riches and prosperity and that the real aim for life should be to seek enjoyment.

"But know one fact. When the Divine Dawn does come down, you will be unable to bear the intense light. The scales on your back will be burnt and charred with its extreme power and you will be forced to flee from creation and go to the nether worlds. Till that time act decisively, but always in a hidden and covert manner, to prepare the ground so that when divine knowledge arrives, it will face a lot of conflict. That is our ultimate goal.

"If human beings do not welcome the Divine Dawn, then the Golden Age will be delayed on the physical plane. If they remain unconscious of the divine descent then we can have more time. This is what we wish for and this will be your task. If human beings remain ignorant about the Gods waking up in them then they will continue to be controlled by the negative forces. But remember: the present opportunity will not come again."

Hearing all these ideas from Kali, Arbuda was full of enthusiasm as he thought of the many new spheres of action where he could become active. But then he became sorrowful. "O Leader of the Age," he addressed Kali. "I have always stood against the values of the Gods. How then shall I save myself and my family when the Golden Age begins? Shall we all be destroyed by the brilliant white light of Truth?"

Kali replied: "As I have told you, you must descend, together with your vast family, to the nethermost worlds. During the Golden, Silver and Bronze Ages, you can relax and live there together with me. Fear of Gods does not exist there as they are banned. I will also be with you during this time."

Then Arbuda was satisfied and he departed to carry out Kali's instructions and realise the goals that Kali had set. Kali was left alone once more. He recalled his other ally, Shani, and as soon as the thought came to his mind, he appeared.

Shani said, "O Kali, Hear how happy the Gods are. Please explain to me what does the Day of the Gods mean. They are all celebrating together. Urjahuti has created Satya Deva, the Lord of Truth."

Kali responded, "Note, Shani, the Gods made these efforts to commence the Age of Truth, the famed Golden Age. Your work will concentrate mainly on how the human beings accept this new development. Will they accept this with joy and acceptance or will they not believe it?"

Shani explained, "I came to visit you so that I can know more about this Age. You have been kept as a captive in the ether by the Rishis, to prevent you from influencing the world. What is my role now in the world? How can I further our common goals? Your work has ceased since you came to mid-space. I heard that when the supreme Creator, Rishi Kashyap, decided to come to the mortal world, he called you here and told you to remain in this mid-space between the higher and the mortal world.

"This is not your time. Even I have realised that. It was only during your time, I could influence the world in a major way. Now, in spite of all my efforts, I do not have such success. You know that the Gods always wish for Dharma in the world. They want to banish me from all worlds. As soon as you left, my influence also started waning. However, I must add that people, at present, do not follow the divine fully. They still worship me in a tiny corner of their hearts. They continue to doubt the Gods. They lack faith, so perhaps I can still have a role. Please guide me as to what I should do.

"I continue to feel hurt that mankind considers me evil, unaware that in their inner thoughts and impulses, they still follow me. They criticise me openly and say that my path is the wrong one. They worship and praise the Gods in public. But in the privacy of their homes they still follow the path that I have shown to them. Their open contempt and disdain rankles me constantly. They never praise or admit their admiration."

Hearing this heart-rending lament from Shani, Kali was astonished. He exclaimed, "Why do you feel sad about these useless and stupid people criticising you? You are almighty at present. Your power is unparalleled and impacts everyone. You should be happy to know that your power makes them suffer. In the depth of their heart, they bow down in front of you. Who has the power to reduce your influence? They who seem to fight for justice and Dharma are still propelled by your power. Arbuda, the Leader of the lower vital forces is still there and is eagerly helping you all the time."

Shani accepted Kali's logic. He also affirmed that Arbuda's influence had assisted him at all times, even though people tried to hide this fact. Still, he was worried and concerned that people did not like him, nor did they worship him. He added, "When I hear Dharma being praised and worshipped in the world, I feel sick and disheartened. Then the deep-seated anger within me becomes strong. With this immense power, a force of destruction is leashed on the world. Under its impact, all life suffers."

Listening to Shani's woes, Kali answered in a reflective and measured manner, "Shani, listen, your Father is Surya, the Sun God, who gives light to the world. Always remember, that his eldest son is Dharma on whom he has lavished all his love and care. All beings, created in this world, perform the task that has been given to them. You have followed the negative path. For this, the Creator has always criticised you. How can you blame the world when they criticise you. This path has been shown by the Creator. The world simply follows him."

Shani acknowledged this fact with a wrenching sorrow in his inner being. "You are absolutely right. My father loves his eldest born Dharma. When he told him to spread his influence in the world, he was full of joy. Do you know how he treats me? He bans me from showing my face in the world and in the heavens. With me, alas, he is never happy. He does not love me at all."

Kali added, "Accept this fact in your inner being. This is the real cause why people do not like you. Forget your despair for the time that is still remaining for us. The long-awaited Day of the Gods is coming soon. For this, they are preparing themselves for their work in the mortal world. They are working hard to dispel the remnants of the night that are still lingering on. They are celebrating the fact that Light has been born again in the world. Later on, the Divine Dawn will be coming down into the mortal world. With that, comes a huge influx of Light and the world will become conscious once again of the Truth. Our task now is to find ways how to delay the onset of this Light? How can we put obstacles in this path?

"You know, human beings always prefer to take action. There is still one way that you could follow. You can darken their thought processes. Slow down the realization of the Divine Dawn in their inner beings. Sow many doubts and disbelief in their minds. My time is coming to an end. My powers are also at an end. But you still can do a lot.

"Mind you, Shani, your work should be done secretly. As you know, human beings are unaware, at present, of the role of universal forces playing in their inner self. They cannot even control their thoughts. They bow down in front of you, and revere you from the depth of their hearts without actually being aware of it. They are offering an ode to the Gods in public, but in their inner being they act exactly as you direct them. They are still under your influence, and, at all times, follow your directions. Accept this reality. Be happy that when they openly pray to the Gods, asking that Dharma should manifest, in reality, they will be following you. Praying for their wishes to be fulfilled, they have only you to turn to for help.

"Where people are sincere, where they really follow Dharma, you have to ensure that they do not achieve their goals easily. On the surface, you should be supporting, encouraging and praising their lofty aims. You should even seem to be helping them, even being with them. But in the background you should try to discourage them.

"In my Age, as you yourself have experienced, humanity is under the influence of the lower vital plane, i.e. under the suzerainty of the serpents. Under this influence, they always worshipped you. They all pray to you for their own selfish reasons. Their minds are propelled by their wish for enjoyment. Their aim is to obtain their own profit and prosperity.

"Having more wealth at their disposal, their desire for enjoyment increased exponentially. As a result, they became victim of dreaded diseases that led to physical suffering. The feeling of desire also increased in each human being. Where there is increasing desire, you are always worshipped. Looking at a woman's beauty, they become overwhelmed by feelings of lust, desire and passion. At that time, their secret wish is how to use and enjoy her body. Emotions of love and respect seldom exist there.

"To this end, men continue to serve you daily. This path was formed by the Creator to further creation. For enjoyment, no knowledge is needed. The only aim is personal happiness. In this way, boys and girls are born in this world. If any problems occur in their lives, they blame their fate. For personal satisfaction, they have no control on their desires and for this they are willing to take any amount of medication. They are even ready to destroy the foetus that has been created through their own lack of control. Such persons always seek your blessings.

"To be able to fulfil these unquenched desires, they dream of obtaining more and more money. For achieving success, they again worship you, O Shani. To this end, they do not hesitate to use deception or even robbery. At that time, the serpents, which have cornered huge amounts of money, provide them with immense riches, thus increasing their greed. When greed expands, and money becomes plentiful, then it leads mankind into all sorts of crimes. You can see, Shani that with your blessings and bounty, their desire for enjoyment has no limits.

"Go and observe the religious establishments and temples, where prayers and worship are supposed to be held. There, all these corrupt practices flourish even more. In my Age, the Kaliyuga, and particularly that portion when they are under the influence of the snakes, they are bound to worship you for the fulfilment of their happiness and satisfaction."

Kali added, "When governments are run in the right manner, then every action brings peace and prosperity to the people. Still, money is necessary at all steps. To defend the country against outside invasion and to provide security to the people, one needs to buy arms and ammunition for the soldiers. Wealth is required also for fulfilling manifold needs. To protect the country against natural calamities, to promote trade and prosperity of the country, money is required. Many times it also happens, that Ministers who are in positions of power in a country, siphon away this money for their own personal use. They then waste it in personal enjoyment. Still they always claim that they perform their duties.

"To be able to judge the present reality, observe it from afar. You will see how Arbuda's powers are clouding the judgement of mankind. The truth becomes evident only if the entire scene is observed from a distance. Mankind bows down in front of Truth, but behind the scenes they do these evil deeds. In public, what people despise and look down upon, those very same actions they do in private. Many others, who are evil and stupid, work towards their own doom by committing such actions.

"So you see, Shani, people are always looking up to you and worshipping you with their actions. They are definitely not following the path of Truth. You are influencing the entire humanity. When they remain quiet due to immense fear, it is not as if they were following Dharma. They are still following you. Really, you should be glad of the power that you are wielding in the entire world."

Finally, Kali added, "When this transitory time comes to an end, you can depart for the nethermost worlds, and live comfortably with me and Arbuda until the Golden Age is over. For us, it will be the night and we can also rest. When the Age of the Gods comes to an end, Dharma will again be influenced negatively. Then, I promise you, my Age will again start. Rest assured that you will once again have a very important role to play."

☆☆☆☆☆

Vishnu's Last Avatar Kalki Heralds the Coming of the Golden Age[8]

Once, the famous Rishi Gautam started to explain the advent of the Devayana and the beginning of the Golden Age to Mahi, the Earth. He said: "Towards the later part of the Kali Yuga, the spiritual knowledge of the East will be under an extremely grave attack. Until then, the eternal religion, the Sanatana Dharma, had been somehow kept alive and safe by the Aryans but it was threatened by the spread of Western science-based knowledge which disparaged the culture and knowledge of the Rishis, and regarded it as, at best, beautiful poetry.

"During that time, fear of death spread everywhere. There were famines, calamities and innumerable diseases. Faced with all these disasters, people could not believe in immortality. They said that if the Gods and the Rishis were immortals, why could they not be seen? It seemed that the only truth that existed was suffering and death; and to avoid them it was necessary to take care of oneself. Everyone wished for happiness;

[8]Devayan/ Vol. 11/Rudra Kalpa/Akhyan Mandala/Hayagriva Varga/ chapter 6-8/pages 3383-3392

but to obtain it, one had to make efforts oneself. Praying for it was useless and one should rather concentrate on the material world and look to scientific discoveries to heal our maladies and make life comfortable. Of course, to achieve all this, one needed money and indeed the rich lived on earth like Gods.

"Now, to demolish the false achievements of this Dark Age that was based on material prosperity, the tenth and last avatar of Lord Vishnu, Kalki, will come to restore balance and harmony on the earth. Then, the world will again be influenced by the holy eternal religion. Knowledge and study through *Tapa* and *Yajna* will become popular. Science has told us many facts about material nature but with so much information available, we become confused and do not know what to believe.

"When the real inner knowledge in us becomes activated, then faith and belief become stronger. These slowly transform into conviction because they are confirmed, day after day, through our experiences and our own work. We are the workers, we are the poet and we ourselves create our own destiny. The knowledge of our inner self will banish our sleep and fatigue, all our actions will be blessed by the divine, every day will be a new world and all that happens will be to our good.

"What Kalki will do will be beyond the imagination of human beings. He will banish fear from the mortal atmosphere, drive away illnesses, including those of the mind, and ward away disasters. He will speak against the differences existing between countries and people. He will tell us the right path to follow to achieve peace and unity, and to remain in amity with each other. He will spread his message everywhere.

"Together with Kalki, the Gods will also play their role. Once again, they will start to influence and work inside human beings. This development had been foretold long before and but it remained a very deep secret. Earth, listen carefully, I will tell you what signs will be there in the beginning of the Golden Age. Please, remember this always. At that time, Pingal Maheshwara will bless the Gods and open their path to the mortal world and help the world to enter into the Golden Age by influencing common human beings from within. And he will do this, through the manifestation of an epic that is unimaginable in its breadth and inconceivable in its depth.

"This epic is the eternal Devayan, the supreme knowledge, and it is also, at the same time, the path that leads us to immortality. Rest assured, Oh Earth, soon Devayan will receive the admiration of the entire world. No one will be able to stop its progress. Then we will see clearly the secrets of the Vedas as well the path to achieve those heights.

"It will be the work of Kalki to spread the message of the Devayan which sings the praises of Satyadeva, the Lord of Truth and that is when the Gods will manifest. Kalki will give the words of the Devayan their form just as Valmiki formed the words to show to the world the real form of Sri Rama, and Vyasa that of Krishna. Similarly, the Kalki avatar will manifest the words of Pingal Maheshwara."

Hearing all this from Rishi Gautam, the Earth replied, "Tell me in detail, Rishi, all that Pingal Maheshwara says? How is it that I do not know about all this? How will the Kalki Avatar manifest in the world?

Rishi Gautam, pray tell me how the facts of Devayan have remained hidden and not become evident to me. It seems to me that I have heard the word, but the detailed text has remained hidden from my view."

Rishi Gautam answered, "In time, many events of earlier history tend to be forgotten. Remember, Earth, the ancient Puranas. They, together with the Vedas, were revealed in the beginning. Now, Pingal Maheshwara has made it evident to us all how Time works. The secrets of the creation of Parabrahman, containing the Gods and the movement of the Time Wheel, will all become evident in front of us. With the movement of Creation, the Time Wheel also moves. In the navel of Brahma, the entire universe exists. It is called the Brahmanda. Within this, is the Lord of Truth, Satyadeva, the intense light and Lord of the Golden Age, and Kali, Lord of the Iron Age, who is the embodiment of utter darkness. The Time Wheel rotates between these Ages, carrying with it the entire creation. Now, it is turning towards the Golden Age, when the entire creation will be conscious of Truth at all times.

"Then, Mahi, you will understand your history, so much of which has been lost with the passing of the Ages. So listen, children of the world, remember, at all times, that you are the children of the Truth. All the creatures of the universe are directed by the World Soul. At the time of the Golden Age, everyone was conscious of their nature. All knew that they were immortal. But with the advent of the adverse forces and evil time, this intrinsic knowledge disappeared and everyone slipped into a state of semi-unconsciousness. People started thinking of themselves as weak and subject to all sorts of pain and suffering. But you will regain your former awareness as the Divine Dawn, Usha, approaches the mortal world. She will remove all suffering and pain.

"All Gods are coming to be with you very soon, O Earth. They will drive away Death and you will become fully conscious and again be immortal. This is what the magnificent epic explains. It tells us about those long-lost memories that will make the entire world again conscious of its history from the beginning of the universe to the end. In this New Age, we will see the world in a new light.

"Earth, you will become like the Mother of Gods and all human beings will be like Gods. They are all children of immortality. So tell them to throw away their bad habits and to remain without fear. Tell me, when eternal joy is their right, then how can they feel sad and depressed? How can they have any suffering when they are children of immortality and all divine powers exist within them?"

Mother Earth was amazed when she heard all this but then Lord Pingal gave to her the secret mantra - the *Aham Rhitam* - and seeing this new path, the Divine Mother became full of joy.

☆☆☆☆☆

Adi Shankara-The Path to Truth-Renunciation or Attachment[9]

In Kerala, South India, a great soul was born. His name was Shankar, also remembered as Adi Shankaracharya. He advised everyone to renounce all material goods, leave their attachment to their loved ones and lead a simple life without any bondage, like a Sadhu. Only then could one concentrate one's entire efforts in attaining divine consciousness. He preached that the world was just an illusion and that men should banish falsehood from their consciousness. False attachment prevents enlightenment and even our attachments to other persons make us lead life like animals with no inner peace. The one and only truth is Brahma, the Creator.

Shankar went to many different parts of India preaching his philosophy and finally reached the renowned city of Kashi, then ruled by an illustrious King from the Pal dynasty, named Tribhuvan. At that time, Buddhism had spread all over India. King Tribhuvan believed in the eight-fold path that Buddha had shown to the world and was an ardent follower. He was

---

[9]Devayan/ Vol. 9/Rudra Kalpa/Lay Mandala/Shankara Varga/chapter 10-16/ 1pages 1741-1751

extremely religious and when he heard that Shankar was coming to visit him to convince him to return back to Hinduism, he thought of a novel way to foil his plans.

When Shankar arrived in Kashi, he found all doors closed to him and thus had no chance to meet the King. He went into a dense forest nearby to think about what to do and there saw a huge palm tree with vessels placed on the topmost branches in which a man was collecting juice from the tree. Shankar was very interested in the whole process and was wondering how the big pots could be brought down when, to his amazement, he saw the big tree bow down to the ground in front of the man as if it was saluting him. Then, it was relatively easy for the man to lift the huge vessels full of juice down to the ground. After the vessels were removed, the tree straightened itself.

Shankar could not believe his eyes. "How you do this?" he asked the man. "Do you have some special powers? Can you teach me?"

The man could tell that Shankar was a Brahmin and he bowed his head in respect. Nevertheless, he decided to test him before imparting his knowledge. "Please come to my house and have your meal with us," he said. "But I must tell you that I am a low-caste. By profession, I am a shoe-maker. Once you have had your meal at my humble abode, then only will I give you this knowledge."

Ignoring the strictures on caste, Shankar willingly presented himself at the lowly shoemaker's cottage. He ate with him gladly and then, bowing down in front of him, again pleaded for his special knowledge. The poor shoemaker was delighted by the respect he had received from this high-ranking Brahmin and happily gave him this knowledge.

Once again, Shankar tried to gain audience with King Tribhuvan, but the gate to the royal court remained shut. Shankar looked around and noticed a huge tree nearby. Using the shoemaker's secret mantra he influenced the tree to bow down enabling Shankar to climb onto its very crown. Then, he used the same mantra again to make the tree bend in the other direction and take him over the wall to the palace and down in front of the king and his courtiers. Everyone was astounded to see this person descending like a God from the heavens.

Then Shankar began to preach. "You are too attached to your high position," he told King Tribhuvan. "And also, you remain ensnared in the illusion of maya or illusion." He turned also to the others present and tried to convince them that they should follow the path of renunciation.

King Tribhuvan accorded Shankar the highest respects and honours and listened to all that he had to say about his philosophy of life. "But before I change my way of life," he told him, "you must first convince the learned scholars of my Kingdom, in particular the famous Tripathak who is well-versed in the scriptures and considered by all as a great intellectual."

Now Tripathak, however, had heard a lot about Shankar's debating skills and was afraid of losing any argument with him. He was scared that he would have to leave his family, his wife and children and live in the forests like a Sadhu. His wife, Ubhaya Bharati, however assured him that she was more than ready to face Shankar and would ensure that he did not challenge her husband in theological debate. When Shankar knocked at Tripathak's door, it was Ubhaya Bharati who opened it. To her surprise, she found there a young man in his early twenties and, which was even more amazing, a strong light streamed from his body as if it was illumined from within.

Ubhaya Bharati was impressed. "Why have you come to my door, sir?" she asked politely. "You have renounced everything in your life. I am merely a woman, who is confined to her own four walls. I think that you do not need any knowledge from me. I am busy with my family and I do not have any new insights to give to you. However," she added, "in my view, I consider your knowledge still not complete. To my mind, you have acquired only partial knowledge."

Shankar in his turn was very surprised to have his knowledge and wisdom questioned, and that too by a woman. "How can you say that my knowledge is incomplete?" he replied. "You do not even know who I am. I have come to your house to discuss some important questions of philosophy with your husband. Please tell him that I have arrived. I have heard from all that he is very intelligent. Now, I see, he has his own family. According to me, without renunciation, there is no knowledge. I have come to discuss this and other matters with him."

"I am his beloved and his wife," Ubhaya Bharti answered. "You can speak with me about everything. In fact, you can see Tripathak only after you have satisfied me. Let us first discuss your knowledge. Once you have managed to defeat me in debate, then only will I disturb my illustrious husband."

Shankara was upset and annoyed. “I think you are very ignorant and stupid,” he said. “Know that I am Shiva, I am Shiva. Pray, tell me what is your knowledge? I need to see Tripathak immediately, without any delay. I am in a hurry as I have to go to visit many places still.”

“From all that I have heard so far, I can only say that you have partial knowledge,” replied Ubhaya Bharti. “You know of the soul, and you say that you are Shiva. The soul exists above the world. It creates the world. That element is without any form, it is like the vast empty space, Sir,” she continued, “Your present body that calls itself Shankar is not without a form. You have taken birth from your mother’s womb. You say the soul is the truth and it does not die, but to maintain your body, you still require food and drink to survive.

“The entire creation manifests itself through the coming together of a man and woman. What knowledge do you have of creation? Tell me, how the child is formed in the woman’s womb and how it enters there. When the soul comes into the body, what knowledge does it have? You say that you are Shiva. But how are you going to prove it? Your voice is coming from your body. Your sentence is coming from your mouth. How did you obtain your body?”

She paused before concluding. “Without a woman, there is no creation. Without creation, a soul cannot express itself. So your suggestion that everyone should renounce their wives, their children and go to the forest has no basis. My opinion is that renunciation as an idea is completely false and should be rejected, as creation can continue only in a family. For these reasons, I say that, at present, you have received only one half of knowledge. When you have received the other half, when you have been together with a woman, then only your knowledge will be complete. At present, you are just like a child. For this reason, you are saying things without any solid foundation."

Shankar was angry within himself at this attack but he kept it well-hidden. "This is neither in our scriptures nor in any book of philosophy," he countered. "If there is any known thesis which expounds this theory, then please let me know. I would like to know the name of this philosophy."

"It is called the Kamashastra," replied Ubhaya Bharti. "It is what Vatsayan propounds."

"All the savants have rejected his theory," Shankar retorted. "It is merely based on sensual enjoyment and does not contain any knowledge that is spiritually gained. Please accept the fact, learned lady, that this is not the truth. Only that knowledge which is contained in the Vedas and the Upanishads is considered divine."

To this claim, Ubhaya Bharti had a very easy answer. She said, "The knowledge of Vedas and the Upanishads has been propagated by men only. To my mind, it is only half knowledge. This world manifests together with the power of women. You have to accept that knowledge is shared between men and women. Only then is it complete. Otherwise it is partial. You have gained all your knowledge from treatises meant just for men and the philosophy that concerns women is unknown to you. The reason is that this practical knowledge can only be obtained when you are together with a woman. For this reason, I say that you have only partial knowledge."

It took a lot of courage for Ubhaya Bharti to say all this to an eminent and powerful person like Shankar. He then became really angry.

"Woman, you are extremely stupid. You are living under a complete illusion. If one's entire life is directed towards sensual enjoyment, then when death comes, one can experience a great sorrow, as we lose our body. We leave our mortal body with our desires for enjoyment unfulfilled. How can enjoyment be experienced without having our bodies and our senses? Can you imagine what happens to us when our desires survive after the body perishes? You are wasting my time. Please call Tripathak, your husband immediately."

Now Ubhaya Bharti was really annoyed. "You are not looking at the facts of creation," she argued. "Not having this knowledge, you are speaking like a child. First experience life, and then expound your theories."

With this exchange of views and with anger on both sides, Shankar decided to leave with his disciples. He promised to come back after a few days when he had gained this experience and spent a few days in Kashi thinking about how to acquire this knowledge. Then he proceeded to Ayodhya where he heard the sound of crying and wailing coming from the palace. Curious to know what had happened, he approached the soldier guarding the gate who told him the sad news that the young King had died suddenly, just a few hours before. Still in his early youth, his untimely death had caused an outpouring of pain and anguish amongst his family and subjects.

Shankar saw in these tragic circumstances an indication of his own future path and continued to think about it as he left the city together with his many disciples. They reached the banks of the river Saryu that flowed through a forest and sat under the shade of a big tree where Shankar began to address his followers. He told them that the Rishis used to sit in such places for meditation and concentration and to teach their students about the Vedas and the Upanishads. He recited his own composition "MohMudgar" (The Hammer to break all Attachment) which perfectly captured the essence of his knowledge. He said that by chanting these words all attachment could be destroyed. The disciples were very happy to receive this knowledge but he had not finished.

"When I went to approach the beloved of Tripathak," he informed them, "she told me that I had no knowledge of creation. I left Kashi intending to acquire this knowledge and considering how to do so. Then, I heard of the untimely death of the young king of Ayodhya and I have now decided that I will enter into the dead King's body. Please guard my body for 3 months after which I shall return. And remember this MohMudgar that I have given you now, for you will have to come to the palace to remind me of it." Saying this, Shankar left his body and entered into the dead body of the King.

The dead king soon showed signs of returning consciousness and slowly sat up. Those around him were amazed and delighted to see him come back to life. They took him back to the palace where the Queen accepted his revival with great joy. In this way, Shankar spent a few days with the Queen and came to understand Kamashastra, the knowledge of human love. But the Queen began to doubt whether he really was the King for his personality seemed to have undergone a great change. Where earlier, he had been fully immersed in sensual enjoyment, so much so that the whole day used to pass in this way, now he seemed detached from everything around him. At times, it seemed as if he had renounced the world and lost his interest in all that he had held dear previously.

Slowly, the Queen became convinced that he who was now her husband was not the same person that had been before and that another soul had entered into her husband's dead body. She ordered her soldiers and her spies to go around the kingdom to see if somewhere a dead body was being guarded. The search continued for many days until one day a spy returned and reported that he had found a group of disciples of the well-known Brahmin, Shankar, in the big forest near the banks of the River Saryu. They were guarding Shankar's dead body and, when he asked them why, they said that their Guru had told them he would soon come back and reclaim his body.

The Queen was convinced that it must have been this realised being, Shankar, who had entered into the King's body. "Go and tell the disciples that the body of their Guru must be cremated immediately," she ordered her officials. "Keeping a dead body for such a long period of time after the soul has departed is dangerous. Diseases can spread very rapidly. Then, take the body immediately to the cremation ground and perform the funeral rites. Also, go around the Kingdom and perform the funeral rites for all those who have died or are in the process of leaving their body."

The Queen's officials did as she had commanded and burnt all those who had died, or even who were about to die, on a funeral pyre. Then, reaching the forest where Shankar's body still lay, they drove away the disciples who were guarding it and took the seemingly dead body to the cremation grounds. Immediately, some of the disciples hurried to the palace where they found Shankar together with the Queen looking after the affairs of the Kingdom. They began to chant the MohMudgar as Shankar had instructed.

"O King, you are busy enjoying your life in luxury and in the company of your wife. Remember your eternal soul which should always be conscious of the presence of the Creator, of Brahma. Why have you left the peace and joy of the ocean of Brahma and why are you attracted towards the beauty of women, who are like the flowers or the swans swimming on the lakes and will take you into the eternal fire? Time will take away your riches, youth, power, position and your ego. Life is like the surface of the waters, soon it will vanish and very soon death will reclaim the body that you have left in the forest."

Hearing this MohMudgar from his disciples, Shankara regained his memories and became conscious that he was not the King. His attachment to the King's body came to an end and he fell down heavily, seemingly dead. Those around him rushed to help the King and tried their best to wake him up but it was of no use.

Meanwhile, the disciples were telling their Guru what had happened and how his own body was about to be cremated. "Hurry to save your mortal body, Oh Guru," they urged. "Or, you will have to pass the rest of your life in the body of the King. You can give so much knowledge to us all. In this present body, you remain without knowledge, attached only to physical pleasures. Surely by now you have gained enough experience of being together with women."

While the disciples continued to chant the MohMudgar, Shankar left the unconscious body of the King; and in the same second entered into his own body which lay on the funeral pyre surrounded by his other disciples, grieving at their inability to save the body of their Guru. Suddenly, the dead body sat up and jumped down from the pyre, took up some sticks and chased off the terrified guards who thought it must be a ghost that had come to attack them. The disciples, of course, knew it was their Guru and bowed down in front of him.

In the palace, the Queen was again immersed in sorrow and those disciples remaining there, tried to console her. "Attachment to another being is only during the lifetime," they sang. "Without life, there cannot be any attachment. Once the body is burnt, then suffering is also forgotten. When the soul is released then, Oh Queen, you should dedicate yourself to the divine. In life, suffering only comes when one considers the loss of one's own happiness, while you can find succour by devoting your love and attention to Brahma, the Creator."

All this, the Queen heard with her closed eyes. She saw that it was due only to illusion or *maya* that one suffers the pain of loss when a person departs and her heart was filled with light and illumination. As her husband was mortal, so death had conquered him. Seeing that the Queen had found peace within herself, the disciples left to join Shankar and the others.

Then, Shankar together with his disciples left Ayodhya and returned to Kashi. He stood at the door of Tripathak's house and called for him loudly. This time Tripathak himself opened the door. Already dressed like a Sadhu, he was ready to renounce his family, his riches and his position. He bowed down and touched Shankar's feet with devotion and respect. Then both of them presented themselves in front of King Tribhuvan and convinced him also to become a sadhu and follow them.

☆☆☆☆☆

Sri Aurobindo and Vande Mataram as a Mantra[10]

In 1872, the future Yogi, Sri Aurobindo, took birth on this earth. He became one of the leaders of the movement for the independence of India from the British rule. Two groups had formed in the Congress Party. One believed that it was best to have a progressive negotiated settlement with the British as then they would willingly transfer power into Indian hands. The other believed that power would have to be wrested from the hands of the British, if necessary even by force. The first group was headed by Surendra and the second one by Aurobindo.

Aurobindo and the members of his group were all young and fiery. When he spoke, he articulated the thoughts and desires of the others. He said: "The English are neither our parents, nor our family elders, that they would give up their power willingly. Their policy is to give us a little bit of power to keep us quiet and contented. But we should not be fooled. We should not forget that they possess powerful weapons, which they would not hesitate to use upon us, should the need arise

[10]Devayan/ Volume 10/Kashyap Mandala/Karma Varga/chapter 5-9/pages 2447-2454

at any time. If they do not like the way we speak, they will not hesitate even a minute to let rivers of blood flow in this land. Do you really believe in your heart that they would give us our independence willingly? Will they just leave our country and let us govern it? Keep always in your mind, that it is only our own people that can give us our rights. The others would just dismiss these as impractical and not easy to implement.

"What we wish to achieve is an immense goal. The actions that we have taken so far are very small and insignificant. To expect that we would achieve our goals at this rate is wishful thinking. If we continue at this pace, the British will remain here forever. We will continue to remain contented with the crumbs that they throw to us and remain in a dream state, expecting the impossible.

"Why do you think they will leave our beloved country and give the administration to us? To my mind, this is absolutely impossible. This can never happen. Many people desire an increasing amount of money and power. Not only that, many of them are interested in the gratification of their senses. This is true of the British, as well. They are also enslaved by their desires. To guard their own property they will try to employ all means.

"Remember my words; they will continue their discussions and conferences with you with a smiling face and a sweet voice. They will offer arguments to convince you of their position. But the minute that you put pressure on them to obtain independence, they will counter it by saying that you are demanding the impossible. They will promise to give you freedom, but only in the future. If the situation deteriorates, do you think that the British will remain quiet? When you try to spread your own convictions to the public, they counter these by proclaiming their own achievements. They will even be ready to bribe people to subvert them and bring them under their influence.

"If we follow this path," he continued, "it will take a hundred years to achieve our goals, and you are definitely not going to have such a long life. And do not forget that the British have the means to unleash a period of terror and will not hesitate to let blood flow in our country. Then, remember what Lord Krishna told Arjun at the battlefield of Kurukshetra, '*Leave your weakness and fear, O Arjun! At a difficult time, why should you be sad, or have fear of death. The soul neither dies nor is ever born. It is eternal; it takes up a body, which it discards when it becomes old and threadbare. The soul cannot be injured by weapons, nor can it be burnt by fire. You are worrying for no reason. In case you leave your body, and if death comes to you, then also you should leave your sorrow.*'"

Aurobindo concluded his argument: "If we continue to beg for our freedom from the British, we will have to remain as suppliants, and we will be cursed for all the ills that befall our country in the future. British rule may even deepen and our voices be silenced. For these reasons, I want to plead with you that we change our policy now and be ready to attack."

Then Aurobindo left Saurashtra and started living in Calcutta. He brought out two publications, Yugantar and Vande Mataram to awaken Indians from their deep sleep. Meanwhile, from a great distance, in fact from a higher plane, Pingal Maheshwara had been observing these new developments. He saw how these daily and weekly newsletters were stirring Indians from their inertia and making them conscious of many issues. Aurobindo's powerful words spread far and wide and it seemed as if a flame had been lit and independence did not seem far away. Secret societies sprung up where heated discussions were held. The Centre in Maniktala was under Aurobindo's brother Barindra, and they started making pistols and even simple bombs. They all knew that if the authorities even had an inkling of their actions, they could face the death penalty.

But Aurobindo's speeches continued to be explosive. "Citizens of Bharat," he said, "why are you indulging yourself in enjoyments when the Asuras are sucking our blood, sitting on our Mother's neck and drinking up our energy? How can you put a morsel in your mouths at such a time? You should concentrate on driving out the devils before you even sit down to eat your food. This is no time to celebrate, to have festivities. Look at Bengal. It is not just a piece of land with earth, rivers and mountains. It has a soul, it is alive.

"Look at what Rishi Bankim is saying in his inspiring book, 'Anandmath'. It is the story of a group of young persons who renounce everything, their families, and their normal lives and live in the forests, completely dedicated to driving away the foreigners who had occupied their country. In this, was a song which was like a mantra. He wrote this great song but only a few listened. But then something happened. As they awoke from their long delusions, the people of Bengal started to look around them, seeking for the truth. In a fateful moment somebody sang the 'Vande Mataram' and in a single day an entire people had been converted to the religion of patriotism. Mother India had revealed herself. Once that vision has come to a people, there can be no rest, no peace, no further slumber till the temple has been made ready, the image installed and the sacrifice offered. A great nation which has had that vision can never again remain under the feet of the conqueror."

This Vande Mataram, he said, should be made a national anthem, but it was also a sacred mantra, revealed to us by Rishi Bankim Chandra, to whom it had probably been revealed by an ascetic, a Sannyasi under whose teaching he was at that time. It was not a new invention, but a revival of an old mantra which had become extinct so to speak by the treachery of one Navakisan. The mantra of Bankim Chandra was not appreciated in his own day but he predicted that there would come a time when the whole of India would resound to the singing of the song.

The word of the prophet was miraculously fulfilled. Listen to these powerful words[1] –

Mother, I bow to thee!
Rich with thy hurrying streams,
Bright with thy orchard gleams,
Cool with thy winds of delight,
Dark fields waving, Mother of might,
Mother free.

Glory of moonlight dreams
Over thy branches and lordly streams, -
Clad in thy blossoming trees,

Mother, giver of ease,
Laughing low and sweet!
Mother, I kiss thy feet,
Speaker sweet and low!
Mother, to thee I bow.

Who hath said thou art weak in thy lands,
When the swords flash out in twice seventy million hands
And seventy million voices roar
Thy dreadful name from shore to shore?
With many strengths who art mighty and stored,
To thee I call, Mother and Lord!
Thou who savest, arise and save!
To her I cry who ever her foemen drove
Back from plain and sea
And shook herself free.

Thou art wisdom, thou art law,
Thou our heart, our soul, our breath,
Thou the love divine, the awe
In our hearts that conquers death.
Thine the strength that nerves the arm,
Thine the beauty, thine the charm.
Every image made divine
In our temples is but thine.

Thou art Durga, Lady and Queen,
With her hands that strike and her swords of sheen,
Thou art Lakshmi lotus-throned,
And the Muse a hundred-toned.
Pure and perfect without peer,
Mother, lend thine ear.

Rich with thy hurrying streams,
Bright with thy orchard gleams,
Dark of hue, O candid-fair
In thy soul, with jewelled hair
And thy glorious smile divine,
Loveliest of all earthly lands,
Showering wealth from well-stored hands!
Mother, mother mine!
Mother sweet, I bow to thee,
Mother great and free!

Translated by Sri Aurobindo

Pingal Maheshwara was astonished to hear the people worshipping their motherland as their Divine Mother, Durga, and immediately sent down an additional force of Truth to reinforce their prayers. To rediscover the divine, people in this book, Anandmath, chant the Vande Mataram and worship the rich and dark soil of their country. All 70 million inhabitants thunder at the same time as they approach their Mother:

"You are the ten-armed Durga, the Devi that we worship everyday in our homes. Release us from the torment of the robbers who have entered your land and show us the path to gain salivation. If we meditate deeply on our Mother we will see Her Divine form with her head decorated by the Himalayas as her crown. With her ten arms, she surveys in all the ten directions.

"Oh Divine Mother, you possess ten arms as you have multiple tasks to accomplish. These arms are holding the ten divine weapons. When they start their attack, they destroy all evils in and around us and drive away the demons. To achieve independence, start torturing the devils. Holding the divine bow in your hands, attack our enemies relentlessly. Only you have the power to conquer evil. See, we have renounced everything in the world and we all are dedicating our lives to follow your directions. Accept us all as your divine soldiers, and provide us with courage so that we can follow your injunctions. Use us as arrows to drive away the evil demons. Assume your form that burns the enemies and that destroys all the devils. To destroy evil, manifest a fire that will land on the bodies of the Asuras. Attack them like snakes and after binding their limbs cut their throats.

"We bow down in front of the Divine Mother and sing odes to her. We worship Her in the same way as we bow down in front of the Gods. O Mother, as the Gods attacked the demons so we beg you to give your power to Bharat. O Divine Mother, seated on the lion, empower the people of Bengal. Reveal the ancient form of Bengal. Look, we are all here in front of you in your temple praying that you appear in front of us. O Durga, as in Ages past, reveal yourself in a human body and when your work is completed, then ascend to heaven. O Mother, we are waiting for you to appear in front of us to grant victory to Bharat. O Mother Durga, who appears in both the peaceful and the violent form, appear before us in Bengal. To be able to achieve freedom in Bharat from foreign forces, O Divine Mother, grant us knowledge, love and power. Bring divine light into our country that is at present immersed in darkness. With your pure light, all darkness will be destroyed.

"Destroy all our bad habits and mistakes, destroy our inherent weakness. Destroy the feeling within us that we are insignificant. Also, destroy the feeling that we cannot do anything, as well as our fears and our selfishness. Remove all these negative feelings that have swamped our country. Provide us with a strong determination; make us generous and always committed to the truth. Drive away from us fear, indecision and hesitation in taking strong positions. Oh Mother Durga, give us again the power to believe in ourselves, to have confidence and to reach our highest goals.

"O Mother, our inherent knowledge has been lost. Bless the entire world with the supramental truth. O Durga, manifest in our divine Bengal. Look at the blessed land where you have given us rich dark soil that that is crowned with the highest peaks, the Himalayas. We pray to you to provide us with truth, art and literature, to give us real knowledge. We all pray at your divine feet, O Mother, please remain with us in this blessed land and provide our bodies with the strength of Yoga. Accept us as your instruments with your own hands. Remove the deep-seated sorrow from within us and light up the lamps of knowledge within us. The youth of Bengal is bowing down at your divine feet. If we receive your blessings, we will guard our devotion and our love towards you and never let it be lost.

"Bless us that our life is devoted entirely to your worship without any disturbances. Let us take the oath of serving you always. O divine Bengal, manifest yourself in front of us. This prayer remains always within me. With this, may we all become conscious of our own power! May our character become godly and full of bravery!"

With such a sense of worship, the youth of Bengal took up the mission of freeing their country. In this way, the mantra *Vande Mataram* lit a divine lamp in the darkness and hopelessness that prevailed at that time. With the divine force and blessings pouring down on it, Bengal arose to drive out the hostile forces from its land and the force of truth spread out from Bengal and woke the whole of India.

☆☆☆☆☆

The Supramental Realisation-When Human Beings Really Become Like Gods[11]

After leading the movement for independence for some years, Aurobindo turned to spiritual matters and remained for a long time in deep meditation. He was convinced that the time had come when the Gods would take birth on this mortal earth. He expounded that in the ancient scriptures there were accounts that the Gods had taken human birth and brought immortality to the world. He called this the 'supramental realisation' and explained how human beings could achieve this state and become supramentalised. He said that the time will come when there will be a race of fully realised beings.

In our earlier scriptures, it is said that supramental beings, who look human, but are radiant with divine light, will come down at the right time to lift us out of the present darkness and transform the earth and all creation so that it is again like heaven. Then, human beings will themselves look like Gods and become immortal like them, their bodies remaining forever young and they will enlighten the world. To achieve this

[11]Devayan/Vol. 11/Bhag Mandala/Prajnana Varga/chapter 1-6/pages 3521 - 3533

blessed state, many tried to work on their bodies and others undertook deep meditation, but most still lived in ignorance, seeking only sensual satisfaction; pain, suffering and disease remained in the world and birth and death continued. When the time is not right, immortality is not possible. It is only in the Age of Truth or the Satya Yuga that it is possible to achieve this state.

So when will this Age arrive? And what is the right path to achieve it? Many have asked these questions. Some wise beings have prayed to Vishwadeva, the World Soul, to tell human beings about the bright future that is awaiting them. They say if only the Gods who are said to be present in the world could materialize, if they could present and manifest themselves, then the truth will become visible.

Vishwadeva saw that human beings possessing the purity of extreme simplicity do exist and knew that these beings will come together and show this state of consciousness in their own bodies and will be called the wise people, the sages. So Vishwadeva, being convinced that this stage will come soon, replied:

"O Human Wisdom, you always worry. Your inner desire is that truth should manifest. Be assured that this will be fulfilled. Look at me. I carry the whole universe within me. I am the one, who will bring immortality down here. I will drive away old age. I will change the appearance of human beings. O Wisdom, in you there has always existed this human feeling. You always concentrate on birth and death and see them coming one after the other. Now observe within yourself, the truth is manifesting. I am the Lord of the World and I am present in all human beings. I am eternal.

For me there is no old age, no pain; and disease or illness cannot attack me. I have neither any needs, nor hunger nor thirst. For me, there is no death."

Then the Human Wisdom replied: "You are eternal, O Vishwadeva, that I can see. But there is still a lingering question in my mind. Please, tell me more about ego. All wise people think that ego is evil and that if only one could abandon this ego, then ignorance will disappear. This is our goal. Your words give us direction so that we can discover how to destroy our egos and cast off our desires. Once we have achieved this, then human beings can become *masters*. This is the yogic austerity (*sadhana)* that has been undertaken by Sri Aurobindo. But, if this is not the right way, then please guide us."

'Listen,' said Vishwadeva. "I am a small part of the Creator who is the source of all. The power, the Shakti, is the force that manifests this creation and I have this power in me. But, if I allow my concentration to wander then I am weak. Ego exists everywhere and can daily lead into the path of ignorance. We have to pay attention to our thoughts. We have to understand that we are in a world where these two paths exist and remember that there is also a higher knowledge that gives birth to the Gods. I am evil - I am good. These are the two ways of thinking in the world. When we think that we are bad, then the evil force affects us, then the asuras increase. We have to continue saying - I am pure, I am filled with the pure power. This is the same power that gives birth to the Gods. This is the same power that Sri Aurobindo told us about and that which leads us to do good deeds.

"Oh Human Wisdom, surrender yourself to me. See how the supramental realization is taking place. Look at how it is spreading light all around and removing attachment and darkness everywhere. It is offering the divine golden light to everyone. Remember always that you are the Truth, the God, and all fear will leave your consciousness, pure immortality will remain in you."

Human Wisdom asked another question. "Your mantra is *Aham Rhitam*, I am the Truth. Please tell me how will it help me?"

"For me, this is the absolute Truth," Vishwadeva replied. "All should become aware of this truth and then your daily work will be done. If your being becomes conscious, then your mind, your consciousness will become enlightened with this feeling. If there is still a trace of ego in the self, if it promotes the feeling of separateness, if it tells you that your work and your mind is different, then you should look at this. Before ego was propelling all actions of the being, but now the divine power is influencing it. Not only that, but this power is remaining at all times within the being. With your efforts, O Wisdom, ego can be eliminated. The ego is part of you, only due to ignorance and lack of complete knowledge, we limit ourselves. With the descent of the higher power, it can be conquered. You will find in yourself a divine joy that will remove all sorrows and tribulations and give you eternal peace."

Saying this, the World Soul finished his explanation. Human Wisdom was happy to hear the great and welcome message that Truth will manifest in those human beings who are aware and conscious in their inner being and are in full control of the thoughts that are coursing through their minds. Wisdom understood that when the mind has attained purity, one hears the words - I am the Truth - *Aham Rhitam* - in one's entire body. This body will then become the domain of the World Soul which will demolish all ignorance. All around in the world will be heard the mantra: I am the Truth, I am the Truth. These words will continue to resound everywhere; and inside each human being the divine wisdom will awake.

Then, a superior intelligence will manifest and, together with the human mind, the world soul will be awakened. Human beings will become supramental and leave behind their mortal consciousness. Old age, diseases and death will become things of the past. In the illumined mind, all activities relating to the mind, body and senses will come from the supramental plane. In this way, slowly the world will attain the supramental consciousness.

God's aim in the world is the same as that of the Rishis who will manifest the divine works with their efforts so that human beings will follow and further this work. The divine mind will be in the human body and will regulate the life force, the mind and the thoughts, and whatever is done at that time will be according to the wishes of the Gods and the Rishis. As humans perform the divine works, their minds will be filled with divine joy, their bodies move according to divine rhythms, and divine light will spread out from them.

Then, human beings will be able to see the truth for themselves with their own mortal eyes. Disbelief will vanish completely from their minds as they see the entire divine world and recognise the divine works, as well as the events happening in other higher planes. With this process, the physical transformation of human beings will be fully achieved. In the innermost depth of their being, they will remain conscious at all times of the divine truth. Becoming aware that the world soul is an integral part of their being, their physical bodies will also change and they will themselves start to look like Gods.

☆☆☆☆☆

Glossary

A

Abhivarta	The King of Rishis, where the Lord of Truth, Satyadeva took birth
Aditi	The Divine Mother, the Mother of all the great Godheads
Aditya	The Sun
Adharma	Ungodly, Anti-dharma (irreligious), Shani
Adharma-Shani	Manifestation of the dark force under the influence of the Sun, Against the Gods, particularly Dharma, his step brother
Agni	The Lord of Fire
Agni devata	The God of Fire, the Lord of the Aspirant Force
Ahalya	The consort of Rishi Gautam
Aham Rhitam	A Mantra to enter into the Golden Age
Akshrapa	The Ocean of Brahman
Akshara-brahman	Brahman as sound
Amrita	Divine wine
Ananda	Bliss
Anandmath	A novel by Bankim Chandra Chatterjee
Angira	One of the seven Rishis, created from the mind of Parabrahman
Angirasa	Sons of Angira
Antariksha	Plane existing between the mental and the physical
Apsara	Dancing girl of heaven
Arbuda	Snake King, Leader of the lower vital forces

Arjun	The third Pandava, the intimate friend of Divine Krishna
Aryaman	A God
Ashwini devata	Son of Surya (the Sun)
Asuraloka	Plane of the Asuras
Asura	Undivine being, Titan, demon, hostile, opponent of the power of God
Asuric	Demonic, like an Asura
Atharvan	Couplet from the Atharva Veda
Atharvan	A Rishi, who was famous for his cures

B

Balkhilya	Rishi who gained enlightenment very young and remained like a young boy
Balrama	Brother of Krishna
Bankim Chandra Chatterjee	A Bengali poet/writer
Bhaga	The Jlane
Brahma	Creator of All
Brahman	The Supreme
Brahmanda	The entire creation, manifested and unmanifested
Brahmanaspati	Another name of Ganapati
Brahmani	Power of Brahma
Brihaspati	Teacher of the Gods

C

Chhanda	Rhythm, Metre
Chhandasa	One who was born with the Vedas, Surya
Chakra	Wheel
Chandra	The Moon, Lord of Ecstasy
Chandra-Vansha	The Lunar Dynasty
Chhaya	Consort of Surya, the Sun, shadow
Chitraratha	The King of the Gandharvas

D

Daksha	A Creator of the Goddess "Devi-Shakti" who has hundred daughters, married to many of the Gods
Dakshayani	Daughter of Brihaspati – married to Putadaksha
Dakshina	Daughter of Parabrahman – married to Brihaspati
Dashratha	King of Ayodhya, Father of Ram, Laxman, Bharat and Shatrughan
Deva	Incarnation of the Supreme Truth, born as a Son of Abhivarta
Devata	Gods, Divine Being
Deva Surya	Deva the Truth as the Sun
Deva Yajna	Sacrificial flame kindled by Satyadeva, for the Golden Age.
Devayana	The Third Epic of India, describes the Four Ages, together with the Movement of the Gods towards humanity and of humanity towards the Gods for the manifestation of the Golden Age.
Devi	Goddess
Dharma	Son of Surya (Sun) also known as Yama
Dirghtama	A Rishi
Dhritrashtra	The blind King of Hastinapur from the Kuru dynasty
Diti	Mother of the Asuras
Divya-deha	Divine body
Durvasa	A Rishi, who took birth under the influence of Rudra, with a violent nature
Dwaipayana	Another name of Vyasa, born in an island
Dwandwa	Diversity, dispute
Dwarka	Capital of Krishna's kingdom
Dwita	Director of the Time Wheel during the Bronze Age
Dwapara	Bronze Age

G

Ganapati	Son of Shiva
Ganesh	Another name of Ganapati

Gandharva	Demi-gods, celestial musician
Gada	Club
Ganga Devi	Goddess of the River Ganga
Gathini	Daughter of Kushika, wife of Pragatha. Mother of Kali, Lord of the Iron Age
Gauribiti	Daughter of Shakti, Vashishtha's Son
Gayatri	Source of all metres, Mother of all chhandas or Vedas
Gopis	Milkmaids
Guru	Spiritual Teacher

H

Hanumana	Monkey devotee of Sri Rama
Hari	A name of Vishnu
Himalaya	Biggest mountain range of India

I

Indra	The King of the Gods, Supreme Being
Indraprastha	Capital of the Pandavas' Kingdom
Irsha	Jealousy

J

Jagat-Surya	Sun of the three worlds
Janardana	A name of Vishnu
Jarasandha	An evil King
Jataveda	Name of Agni
Jiva	A living being

K

Kakshivan	A Rishi
Kala	Time
Kalachakra	Time Wheel, the holder of the three worlds, the bhuvanas
Kâli	The Power of Rudra

Kali	The Lord of the Iron Age, the Kali Yuga
Kali Yuga	Period of Time influenced by Kali
Kalki	Lord Vishnu's tenth Avatar
Kalpa	A Day of Brahman consisting of the Four Ages
Kama	Short form of Kamdeva, also desire, passion
Kama Shastra	A treatise on desire and passion
Kansa	An evil and brutal King, who ruled over Mathura
Kanva	One of the Seven Rishis, who came out from the mind of the Parabrahmana.
Kanveya	Son of Rishi Kanva
Kashi	Name of an ancient city, also called Varanasi
Kashyapa	A Rishi, Father of the Gods, who also came out from the mind of Parabrahman, the great Creator
Kavi	The Seer, Poet
Krishna	Vishnu's incarnation during the Bronze Age
Kurukshetra	Battlefield of the Mahabharata War

L

Lanka	A country, an island near the south of India
Lakshmi	Daughter of Brihaspati and consort of Lord Vishnu

M

Madhusudan	A name for Lord Krishna, Vishnu
Mahakâla	The Great Time, Shiva
Mahakâla	Pingala A creative aspect of Shiva, a poetic form
Mahakâla-Rudra	A destructive aspect of Shiva
Mahalaxmi	Power of Vishnu
Mahamâya	Great attachment, Durga, Maheshwari
Maheshwari	Power of Maheshwara
Mahi	The Earth
Mantra	The words which when repeated constantly help in attaining inner consciousness, power, peace,

	ananda, etc.
Manu	The Creator
Maya	Attachment
Meghapuri	High peak in the Himalayas
Mohini-maya	An attachment that charms
MohMudgar	by Shankaracharya, (Hammer to break attachment)
Mitra	God who promotes harmony, creates in us a happiness Of mind and feeling, guards life.
Mitra-Varuna	The twin Gods for the infinite wideness and purity of the being
Mrityu	Death, Daughter of the Sun from Sandhya-chhaya
Muladhara	The lowermost part of the body, one of the chakras

N

Nakta	The dark existence
Naraka	Hell
Narayana	The manifested cosmic existence, who exists throughout all creations

O

Om	The primal sound, Aksharabrahman

P

Padma	Lotus
Panis	The demons
Parabrahman	The unmanifested eternal existence
Parjanya	The God of Rain
Parvati	Daughter of Parvat Himalaya, Consort of Shiva.
Pingal	The Poetic existence, the poetic form of Maheshwara
Prakriti	Nature
Prithivi	Earth
Pusha	The Sun as the Divine Power

R

Rajarshi	King who remains as a Rishi, detached from worldly enjoyment
Rakshasa	Anti-divine, Titan, demon
Rakshasi-force	Power of the anti-divine, hostile forces
Rama	An incarnation of Vishnu, the Son of Dashratha
Ravan	A demon, King of Lanka, who was killed by Lord Rama
Rik	Lines from Rigveda
Riti	The right way, direction
Rigveda	One of the four Vedas, the most ancient scripture
Rishi	A Seer
Rishhta	Destruction
Rukmini	Consort of Lord Krishna
Rudra	The destroyer, a destructive form of Maheshwara
Rudrani	The female form of Rudra

S

Sama	Lines from Samaveda
Samaveda	One of the four Vedas, India's most ancient scripture
Santana Dharma	Eternal religion
Sandhya	Evening, negative force always helping Nakta
Sangya	Wife of Surya
Sanjay	Disciple of Rishi Vyasa, who could see at a distance
Saryu	Name of a river that flows near Ayodhya
Sati	Daughter of Daksha, married to Shiva
Satya	Truth
Saurashtra	located in the State of Gujarat
Shakti	Son of Vashishtha
Shanti	Peace, Daughter of Yama
Shani	Saturn
Shankaracharya	Also called AdiShankracharya, who propagated Advaitism, non-duality

Shatakratu	Indra, the King of Gods, who had performed 100 yajnas
Shishupal	The evil nephew of Lord Krishna
Shiva	One of the Trinity
Shukracharya	Teacher of the Asuras
Siddhidata	God of poetic realisation for the Truth, Other names are Heramba, Ganapati, Ganesh, Brahmanaspati etc.
Snake	One with undivine power
Supramental	Sri Aurobindo's name for Maharloka of the Upanishads
Supramental	Realisation When human beings become like Gods
Surya	Sun, Lord of Mental Truth
Surya Sangya	Power of the Sun, consort of Surya also known as Usha Sangya
Swar	Heaven, the mental plane
Swarga	Heaven

T

Tapa	Religious austerity
Tapasya	Religious austerity, penance, discipline for the achievement of power
Treta	Director and holder of the Time Wheel, under his guidance we have the Silver Age, (Treta Yuga)
Tretayuga	Silver Age
Tribhuvan	A King of Kashi, aBudhist
Tripathak	A learned Brahmin
Twasta	The Divine Architect

U

Ubhaya Bharati	Wife of Tripathak, who dared Shankracharya
Usha	Divine Dawn, Daughter of Satyadeva
Usha-Sanjana	Power of the Sun on the mental plane, an awakening conscious power

V

Vaishnavi	Power of Vishnu
Vajra	Weapon of Indra
Vak	The daughter of Rishi Aptya and Ambhrini
Valmiki	Poet of Ramayana
Vande Mataram	National anthem of India, name of a daily and a weekly publication by Sri Aurobindo
Varuna	God who brings to us the infinite space of the divine soul and its elemental purity
Vashishtha	Rishi, son of Mitra-devata
Vasu	God of riches
Vasudeva	Another name of Krishna
Vasuki	The Snake King who holds the creation on his head in the subtle world
Vayu	Lord of the Wind, the Life Force, Commander of the Divine Forces
Veda	The unique spiritual authority
Vedic	Authority of spiritual Truth
Vibhishan	The brother of Ravan
Vidarbha	An ancient Kingdom in India
Vinayaka	Son of Shiva, another name of Ganapati
Vipriti	The wrong path
Vishnu	The Protector, who maintains and protects the world
Vishwadeva	The Sun, The World Soul
Vishwakarma	Son of Swar-Bhuvana
Vishwamitra	Rishi, Son of Gathi Kaushika
Vishwavasu	King of the Gandharvas, the celestial musicians
Vritra	The Leader of the Asuras, son of Diti
Vyasa	The poet who wrote Mahabharata, the second epic of India

Y

Yajat	Couplet from the Yajurveda, one of the four Vedas
Yadavas	Krishna's family, clan
Yajna	A sacrifice, the flame of sacrifice
Yama	Eldest Son of Surya, the Sun
Yamaloka	The world of Yama
Yudhisthir	The eldest Pandava
Yuga	Age
Yugantar	A weekly publication by Sri Aurobindo

☆☆☆☆☆